Books by Cassie Hayes

GOLD RUSH BRIDES SERIES
The Beginning
Emmy

THE DALTON BRIDES SERIES
The Drifter's Mail-Order Bride

The Drifter's Mail-Order Bride

-The Dalton Brides-

Cassie Hayes

The Drifter's Mail-Order Bride

The Dalton Brides

ISBN-13: 978-150556034
ISBN-10: 1505560535

Cover art by Kim Killion
Edited by Kirsten Osbourne & Kit Morgan
Interior design by Cassie Hayes

www.CassieHayes.com

Give feedback on the book at:
cassie@cassiehayes.com

Facebook.com/AuthorCassieHayes

First Edition

Printed in the U.S.A

For the Bonnie in all of us.

-Prologue-

THE BROTHERS

Walton Dalton stood in the middle of his land, knowing he'd found his place in the world. The two sections next to his were both open, and he was staking claim for his brothers. The three of them would own a huge section of Texas dirt, and they would ranch it together.

Walton was the oldest of three brothers. They didn't like to be reminded that he was the oldest though. With only fifteen minutes difference between him and his brother, Nate, and twenty-five minutes between him and Bart, they preferred to all think of themselves as the same age. They weren't though. Walton was always aware of his burden as the eldest. He had to be the strongest, fastest and best of the three, so that he could live up to what was expected of him.

He hadn't built his house yet, so he sat down right there in the dirt to write letters to his brothers, asking them to join him. He knew they would. He'd always been the ringleader of the three of them, and even as adults, he was certain he could convince them ranching was the way for them to gain wealth and happiness.

Rather than writing two different letters, he just wrote one and copied it for the other. When he was finished, he had two letters that read the same.

My Dear Brother,

I'm writing you from a section of land that I'm about to begin homesteading in north Texas. The two sections beside me are available. I'd like for the three of us to claim this land and build a ranching empire here in the Lone Star State. We could have land for as far as the eye can see, and the prairie here is so flat you can see a long way.

I'm about a half day's ride south of a town called Weatherford, which is west of Fort Worth. If you get to the area, people will know me. No one forgets a Dalton.

I hope you'll consider joining me here, because I need you both. There's enough work for twenty men, but between the three of us, I know we can do the

*work of thirty. Remember what Pa always said?
"When you three team up, nothing can stop you."
The local ranchers won't know what hit them once
the Dalton brothers make their mark.*

*I'm going to start building my cabin. When you
two get here, we'll build a couple more houses and
get us some ladies. It's time.*

*Don't take too long to get here. Land is going fast.
Sincerely,
Walt*

He folded both of the letters and got to his feet. His
spirited stallion danced away from him, as if he was
trying to get him to not settle down. "We're here to
stay, Spirit. No more wandering for us."

Walton and Spirit had done more than their share
of traveling. He had spent the last ten years as a
cowboy, learning the ins and outs of ranching. He was
finally ready to start a life, and he was going to do it.

He swung up onto Spirit and rode him into town. It
was an hour to the closest small town of Wiggieville,
but he knew that with his two brothers' help, they
would soon have a bustling town right there. He could
picture it already.

For the life of him, Bart Dalton couldn't figure out
how his brother Walt had tracked him down. He'd

only ridden into the bustling city of San Francisco the day before, after all, and hadn't even planned on stopping there. How in high heaven did Walt know to send a letter to the San Francisco post office before Bart even knew he was going there?

Bart had been on his way from running an apple-picking crew in the Yakima River Valley in the Washington Territory to a new California village called Hollywood when he hooked up with a couple of other drifters like himself. They said they were headed for Frisco, so he tagged along. It wasn't like he had any pressing business in Hollywood, he just thought the name sounded nice. He could almost see massive groves of holly trees surrounding the little community.

As he thought back on his last letter to his brothers — he always wrote one and just copied it for the other — he recalled saying something about California. But that was months ago. As far as Walt and Nate knew, he could have come and gone by then.

But it had always been like that with them. No matter how much distance separated them, they always seemed to know in their gut what was happening with the others. Like that time Walt got bucked from a horse he was trying to break and got a concussion.

Bart had been dealing faro in a Kansas City gambling hell at the time, and an overwhelming urge to sleep came over him. Somehow he knew Walt had been injured so he walked right out of that hell, jumped on his trusty horse Roamer, and rode east in the direction of St. Louis.

By the time he arrived several days later, Walt was up and around, and didn't seem the least bit surprised Bart had shown up. Nate arrived a few hours later. They all had a good laugh, and spent a few days reminiscing and catching up before Bart's feet started itching to get back on the road. That was the last time he'd seen his brothers, and he missed them something fierce.

Being triplets, they'd always been close but, aside from his brothers, no one ever let Bart forget he was the youngest, even though it was only by minutes. Walt was the bossy older brother and Nate was the no-nonsense one. Everyone expected Bart to be the wild one of the bunch, the irresponsible younger brother, and he was all too happy to oblige.

He'd get into all sorts of trouble and blame it on his brothers. Of course, they did the same to him, so it evened out in the end. He pretended it was all in good fun, but deep down he felt empty, like something was missing. It was like he hadn't yet found his true identity, and everyone's expectations — or lack of them — were holding him back from discovering it.

As he and his brothers grew older, he felt stifled at his family home in Oregon City. His brothers seemed perfectly content helping out around the dairy farm, but Bart knew there was so much more out in the world than milking cows and shoveling manure. He wanted to see it all. Maybe once he saw everything there was to see, he'd settle down and live a 'normal' life, but until that day, he'd never be truly happy.

The day after their seventeenth birthday, Bart woke up ready to break the news to his brothers: He was leaving and didn't know when or if he'd ever see them again. He was giddy with excitement but also heartbroken at the idea of leaving them.

They were a part of him and he was having trouble imagining life without them, but he had to do this. As much as he wanted them to come with him, he had to strike out on his own and find that elusive thing that was missing from his soul.

His gut churned as he crept through the quiet house in the early morning hours. He'd get Roamer saddled and packed, then go wake his brothers. If he was lucky, he'd be able to sneak away without waking his folks. Ma would have a fit and Pa might refuse to let him go. He longed to say goodbye but it would be too risky.

Stepping into the barn, he was stopped in his tracks by the sight of his entire family — Ma, Pa, Walt and Nate — standing around an already-saddled and fully loaded Roamer. Tears were streaming down Ma's plump cheeks, and Pa had a comforting arm wrapped around her shoulders. Walt had a worried look on his face and Nate just looked irritated. Only Pa was smiling, even though it held a twinge of sadness.

"How did you know?" Bart stammered in surprise.

Pa tilted his head at Walt and Nate. "Your brothers told us. You didn't tell them?" He chuckled and shook his head. "Figgers."

"I packed you several days worth of food," sniffled his mother. "Don't eat it all at once. I can't stand the thought of you starving out on the trail."

"Yes, Ma," he whispered, humbled at his family's support and love. Why hadn't he trusted that they would understand?

Walt sidled up to him and slapped him on the back. "You'll be fine out there, Bart, but you know if you ever need anything, me and Nate are here for ya."

"I know, brother."

As irritated as Nate looked, he still pulled Bart into a fierce hug. "Don't be stupid."

Bart smiled. It was an old joke between them, going back to when they were little kids. He returned his brother's hug, and soon his whole family had their arms wrapped around him.

Pa was the first to pull away. Clearing his throat of emotion, he croaked, "Sun's fixing to come up, son. Best you get while the getting's good."

Bart gritted his teeth as he rode out of the barn, willing himself to not look back. If he looked back, he might change his mind, and the last thing he wanted was to be stuck in Oregon City for the rest of his life.

Leaving his family behind was the hardest thing he'd ever had to do. And in the ten years he'd spent rambling around the country, it remained at the top of the list.

Rereading Walt's letter, Bart bristled a bit at the commanding tone. Walt always assumed the others would do whatever he told them to, like he was their ringleader or something simply by virtue of being a few minutes older. Bart had spent much of his youth rebelling against his oldest brother's overbearing ways, and he was amused to find the instinct was still there. Some things never changed.

"Whatchya got there, Bart?"

Bart was startled out of his reverie by one of his latest riding companions. Chuck was his name, and he was as shifty a drifter as Bart had ever met. And he'd met a lot. He would never dream of doing business with the man, but Chuck was pleasant enough to pass the time with on the trail.

"Oh, just a letter from my brother, inviting me to settle near him in Texas," Bart replied, carefully folding the letter and slipping it into an inner pocket he'd had sewn into his duster.

"Oh, yeah?" Chuck's eyes sparkled as he leaned back against the wall of the post office next to Bart. "I hear they're giving away land left and right out there.

Whereabouts is he settling?"

There was an unspoken code among drifters like them: Never ask personal questions. Too many men were running from something, and all were suspicious by nature, so it was best to keep your questions to yourself.

Obviously Chuck hadn't learned that lesson yet.

"North, I think," Bart evaded.

Chuck took the hint and nodded sagely, as if that explained everything. "You goin'?"

The man's question took him by surprise. He honestly hadn't even thought about it. He'd been too wrapped up in memories.

"I dunno." And he really didn't. He'd been moving around so much over the years that he didn't think he'd know how to sit still for very long, even if he was so inclined.

Which he wasn't.

But something tugged at his insides, remembering the day he rode away from his family. He'd do anything for them, and now Walt was asking for his help. *I hope you'll consider joining me here, because I need you both.* That was as close to begging as Walt ever got.

Bart was honestly surprised that his brothers hadn't married and settled down by now. They'd both always been more traditional and down-to-earth than he had ever dreamed of being — or ever wanted to be.

But at 27, they were a bit overdue in starting their

own families. He ached for them a little because they'd both always talked about having a bunch of young'uns running around. He didn't really understand it but he felt bad for them that they didn't have it yet.

Resolve settled in his belly like a glowing coal. His brothers would do anything for him, and had already helped him out of more jams than he cared to think about. Walt was right; it was time. Time to return the favor.

He'd ride out to Texas and help Walt and Nate set up their ranch, even if it took a year or two. It was the least he could do. When everything was rolling along, and his brothers had a couple of nice wives — maybe even some babies — he'd leave his portion to them and continue his search for whatever was missing in his life.

"'Scuse me," he mumbled to Chuck and strode back into the post office.

Walt,
You can count on me, brother.
Bart

"Get him, Nate!"

A growing crowd of townspeople and cowhands cheered as Nate Dalton landed face first in the dirt. He rolled to his back and, with lightning speed — at least it felt like it, considering the blow he'd been dealt — climbed to his feet to face his opponent. The dirty chuck-eater clobbered him with a piece of firewood, and even now held it before him like a shield.

"Seems we have a difference of opinion," Nate told him as he wiped away the blood trickling down one side of his face. This had to be the worst cattle drive he'd ever been on.

The Easterner, a man Nate figured had no business changing the price per head, swallowed hard and raised the wood as if to hit him again. The difference was, this time he faced Nate instead of sneaking up on him like he did when he'd struck him the first time.

"As Mr. Meyer's du...duly appointed representative..." he stammered, "I must ask you to concede to the new price given."

Nate shook his head against a bout of dizziness, and hoped he didn't have a concussion like the one his brother Walt did a few years back. For a scant second he wondered if his two brothers would show up to check on him as they'd done for Walt.

The thought was lost however when the good-for-nothing dandy took another swing at him. Nate ducked and dodged, and blocked the next blow with one fist as he punched the low-life in the face with the other to send him sprawling. "I'll do my business with Mr. Meyers, if you don't mind."

The man didn't get up. In fact, he didn't respond at

all. Nate stared at him a moment as Sam Wheeler, one of his drovers, slapped him on the back. "You showed him!"

Nate leaned forward and peered at the unconscious form. At least he hoped he was unconscious. He didn't hit him that hard, did he? "Where's Meyers? How come he sent this idiot for me to deal with?"

"He's at his ranch. I hear tell from folks down at the post office his wife is having a baby. That's why this yellow-belly is in town."

"This yellow-belly tried to gouge the price per head. Now I'll have to ride out to the Meyers' ranch to get our business done."

Sam looked at the man on the ground. A couple of their fellow cowboys tried to get him to come around by slapping the side of his face a few times. "Maybe you should take this fool back with ya and tell Mr. Meyers what he did?"

"Won't have to," Nate said. "This is a small town, with enough people here to let Meyers know what happened. I'll wager this duffer to be out of a job come suppertime."

"Oh, good point," said Sam as he reached into his pocket. "I almost forgot, here's a letter for ya."

"A letter?"

"Yeah, it's from your brother. He wants ya to come to Texas."

Nate's eyes narrowed. "You read my mail?"

"No help for it! There's a tear in the envelope, see?" he said and pointed. "Is it my fault if'n the letter fell out?"

Nate rolled his eyes and shook his head in exasperation. It hurt. He winced as he touched his wound and blinked a few times to clear his vision. He was tired of dealing with ranchers who didn't know how to run their business or make a good profit. He hoped whatever Walt wrote didn't add to an already disastrous cattle drive. He unfolded the letter and studied it, but the words were too blurry for him to read. Not a good sign.

"Looks like the dandy got ya a good one," said the grizzled cowhand as he stared at Nate's head. "Want me to read your letter for ya?"

"I'll be fine, go make sure that idiot is still alive, will ya? And then tell the rest of the boys to wait for me. I'll be back."

"Where ya goin'?"

"Post office." He strode past Sam and headed down the street. He didn't get far when another bout of dizziness hit, and he slowed his pace to keep from falling over. He'd been hit in the head before, be it from a fist, a kick, or the occasional hard object, but this particular hit, coupled with Walt's letter, managed to do something Nate hadn't yet. It knocked some sense into him. "Sense" being the operative word.

Nate used to have his share of good sense at one

time, the type other men respected and sought out so they could benefit too. Nate, being as sensible as he was, gave his advice freely. Not only did he give it, he was willing to receive it.

Except for a piece of advice given him by his last employer, one Thomas Adams, who advised Nate to stay away from his daughters, or else. The "or else" meant Nate would decorate a cottonwood come morning if Mr. Adams found any of his precious daughters compromised.

Nate wasn't stupid and, lucky for him, wasn't attracted to any of the four women. This made it easy to stay away from them. Keeping them away from him, on the other hand, was another matter.

Two of them snuck into the bunkhouse one night. A third rode out to where he and some of the men were branding cattle. If he'd listened to his good sense, he'd have high-tailed it off the Adams' spread pronto. But no... Instead, Lucretia, the fourth and most aggressive of the bunch, launched herself at him the same night in the foyer of the ranch house. She flung her arms around his neck and kissed him as her father came down the stairs.

Nate barely escaped with his life.

But his ordeal with the Adams sisters was behind him, and he wanted to keep it that way. If there was one thing he couldn't stand, it was a forward female trying to rope him into matrimony. He would marry when he was good and ready, not to mention settle down.

Nate reached the post office and leaned against the door a moment before going in. By now his head throbbed something awful. He unfolded Walton's letter and took another stab at reading it. It wasn't easy, but he managed. After several moments he refolded the missive and stuck it back into a shirt pocket.

"Texas," he muttered to himself. "Looks like you found yourself a sweet deal, big brother." But was he ready to join him?

"Good Lord!" A woman cried to his left. "What happened to you?"

Nate stared at her, a bemused look on his face. She pointed to his head and gasped. "Oh, yeah. Sorry ma'am. I...got cut ...shaving."

The woman shook her head and made a tsk, tsk, tsk, sound. "You'd best get that taken care of. What were you doing? Trying to shave your head with an ax?"

"A piece of wood, actually," Nate said drily. "Bad barber." He turned and headed for the postmaster.

"Yes?" said a wiry little man behind the counter. He peered at Nate over his spectacles and gasped louder than the woman. "Egad! You're bleeding!"

"I've been informed. Do you have any other mail for me? The name's Nate Dalton." It would be like

Sam to bring only the one letter and leave everything else. The postmaster grimaced one more time before he turned to search for any remaining mail.

Nate and the other drovers only came to Fountain, Colorado once every couple of months. As it was more frequent than other places he'd been cow punching, it was as good a place as any to have his mail sent.

"No sir, Mr. Dalton," the postmaster announced as he turned around. "Nothing else here. Lucky you came into town when you did, that letter arrived only a week ago."

"Much obliged," said Nate as he turned and headed for the door. As he stepped onto the boardwalk a thought struck. After he sold his employer's stock, collected the money, and headed back, he wouldn't have another chance to answer Walton's letter until the next time they brought in more cattle.

He stared at the dirt in the street in indecision. He could still taste the same dirt in his mouth. He let out a weary sigh, took his brother's letter out of his pocket, and stared at it a moment.

"Texas ..." he mused. Walt wanted to settle down, start an empire, not to mention a family. Was he ready to do that?

A man crossing the street caught Nate's eye. The man was heading toward the post office. Nate reached out and stopped him before he could go inside. "Hey mister, where's the doctor in this town?"

"Go down to the end of the street, turn left, and you'll find him. I think he just got back from the Meyers' ranch." He looked at Nate and let out a low whistle. "I think you'd best hurry and have him tend ya." The man shuddered, pulled out of Nate's hold, and went into the post office.

Nate watched him go, before he looked in the direction he'd indicated. As he started off, he wondered if Bart answered their brother yet. Would he be ready to settle down? Of the three, Bart had the worst case of itchy feet.

Nate could wander as well as the next, but he at least stuck in one place for a while before moving on. Sometimes he'd stay in one spot a couple of years. Bart was lucky to stay in one place a couple of months. But in his gut, Nate knew Bart had answered their brother's call.

He reached the doctor's house, stuffed Walt's letter into his pocket again, and went inside.

"Jumpin' Jehoshaphat!" An elderly man cried when he saw him. "What happened to you?"

"Never mind, are you the doctor?" asked Nate. "I need me a piece of paper and something to write with. I got a letter here needs answering."

"Letter? I'd say let it wait, son. That gash on your forehead needs tendin'. Let me get a few things and I'll fix ya right up."

"My letter needs tending more than I do."

"What's so important it can't wait until after I fix your wound?"

Nate gave him a broad smile. "Cause I gotta let my big brother know I'm gonna settle in Texas!"

The doctor gawked at him, shook his head, and went to fetch him paper, pen, and ink.

Dear Walt,
Count me in.
Nate

Walton worked hard to build a small house while he waited for his brothers' replies. Twice a week he would ride into town for fresh supplies and see if there were any new letters.

Finally, more than a month after he'd mailed his letters there was one from Bart. Walton read it right there in the store and smiled. One of his brothers would be there any day, and they'd start building their empire. The Daltons were going make their mark on Texas.

It took another week before he received a later from Nate. He was coming, too. All of the brothers would soon be together.

By the middle of August, they had constructed

three small cabins in the middle of the property, and they had a growing herd of cattle. Walton had noticed an advertisement in the local paper for mail order brides. He knew Bart had no intention of marrying, and Nate wanted to wait until the ranch was more stable, but they were younger than him, after all. By the time their brides arrived, they'd understand his need to have a family.

After their supper of beans and beans that evening, Walton's brothers went home and left him alone as they did every night. He sat at his small table and wrote a letter.

Dear Miss Miller,

My brothers and I have a large ranch about an hour out of Wiggieville, Texas. We've built three houses here and have the start of a good herd of cattle. That means we're ready to marry. We're identical triplets, so we're all about six foot with brown hair and brown eyes. We're strong men and perfectly capable of providing for brides and any little ones that may come along.

We're twenty-seven, and would really like women between the ages of eighteen and twenty-six. Looks aren't terribly important, but they need to be willing to work hard and cook well. We're all sick of eating our own cooking.

I look forward to your response.

Sincerely,
Walton, Nate and Bart Dalton

Walton folded the letter and set it aside. He'd mail it when he went to town for supplies the next morning. Soon, they'd have women doing their cooking and cleaning. Not to mention keeping them warm at night. Walton smiled. He liked the idea of a little lady to keep him warm at night more than he was willing to express.

THE SISTERS

Gwen Blue hurried through the dark streets of Beckham. Why had Gertie wanted to meet her so late at night? She was going to be married to Stanley in just a couple of weeks, so she wasn't certain why the woman would want to meet her most bitter enemy at all, but she'd go. The letter had said something about mending fences, which sounded good to Gwen after a lifetime of hateful rivalry.

When she arrived at the schoolhouse where they had once been classmates, she looked around. She'd always loved this playground, but it seemed different at night. It was scary.

Stanley stepped around the schoolhouse and walked to her. "Oh, Gwen, I'm so glad you've come!"

Gwen looked at her old suitor with surprise. "What are you doing here?" Stanley stepped closer to her, and Gwen took a step back. "I was supposed to be meeting Gertie."

Stanley reached out and touched her cheek. "I wrote that letter, Gwen. I can't marry Gertie when I'm still in love with you. I never should have broken off our courtship. Will you forgive me and give me another chance?"

Gwen stared at him in disbelief before finally shaking her head. "First, let's get one thing straight. You did not break off our courtship. I did. I broke it off when I saw you looking at Gertie's bosom after church one day. Second, you brought me here under false pretenses? No, I will not forgive you. No, I will not take you back. You need to marry Gertie like you promised. If you don't, everyone will always know what a cad you are. Don't contact me again."

Gwen was practically shaking with anger as she spun on her heel to go back home. She'd thought she and Gertie would be able to put their past behind them. No, it was just Stanley being selfish once again.

Stanley put his hand on Gwen's shoulder and spun her back around. "You know you still love me!"

He crushed his lips to hers, and she stomped on his foot to get him to release her. How had she ever thought she loved this man? "Let go of me, you fool!" She tore away from him and rushed away. She never should have come.

Two days later at church, Gwen sat with her sisters, Bonnie and Libby, wondering why the ladies of the church refused to speak to her on her way to the pew. Some even moved their dresses out of the way to keep them from touching her. She felt like a pariah, and she didn't even know what she'd done to be treated that way.

Bonnie and Libby had received the same treatment for the most part, but no one had avoided getting touched by them. Gwen had always been the most popular girl in their entire congregation, with men flocking around her, but that had changed as well. Even her current sweetheart, Norbert Rumfield, had refused to speak to her. She didn't know what people thought she'd done, but she certainly hadn't. Whatever it was.

Their mother took her seat on the other side of Bonnie, and leaned over glaring at Gwen. "Why do all my friends think you're pregnant?"

Gwen stared back at her mother, her mind spinning. Pregnant? Yes, she'd probably kissed a few more boys than she should have over the years, but she'd never even let one of them touch her breast. No, she wasn't pregnant. Who would say that?

"I have no idea, Mama. I'm not. I swear!"

Bonnie and Libby snickered. They loved it when Gwen was in trouble. She always shamed them because she was always kissing all the boys. There weren't enough men in town when Gwen was around.

Sarah Blue looked back and forth between her oldest and youngest daughters. "What are you two laughing about? Rumors also say the two of you were seen kissing the same boy! Where did I go wrong?"

Bonnie and Libby exchanged glances. "Never!" Bonnie exclaimed. "I've never even kissed one man, Mama."

Libby shook her head. "Gwen always beats us to the boys. We never get a chance to kiss them."

Gwen glared at Libby. "I can't believe you just said that! I hate you!" She stood up and ran out of the church. People were saying mean horrible things about her, and she wasn't about to put up with it.

When she got outside, she wiped away her tears. Leaning against the back of the church, she sighed. Why were people always willing to believe bad things about her? No, she wasn't an angel and never pretended to be. But she wasn't a whore, and that's what people were making her out to be, and it just wasn't fair.

She did just as much volunteer work as the next woman and worked hard to make certain she always looked her best. It wasn't like she was shallow, she just felt like the orphans in town deserved to see a pretty woman and not one with her hair all down around her shoulders looking scraggly.

She sat there for a minute before she realized her nemesis from her schooldays, Gertie Landry, was glaring at her. "I heard you kissed my beau in the park late one night this week," she sneered. "He's still marrying me, though."

Gwen looked at Gertie. Had she started the rumors? "I didn't kiss him. He forced a kiss on me. I told him I'm not interested in renewing our relationship. That's what he wants, you know. He wants me to take him back so he won't have to marry you."

Gwen knew her words were mean, but there were times when she just couldn't hold back, and just looking at Gertie had made her angry for years. Ever since the other girl had pushed her in the mud when she was on her way to her first church social. She hadn't been able to clean up enough, and Gertie had danced with her beau. Spiteful girl.

Gertie walked closer. "That's not true! He told me what happened. You saw him and ran to him in the park, demanding he break off our engagement, and then you flung your arms around his neck and kissed him. You're a tramp, Gwen Blue!"

"Did you start the rumors about me being pregnant?" Gwen stood up and faced the other girl.

"Now you won't be able to entice all the men you meet." Gertie smirked at Gwen.

"People are going to know you lied."

"By then I'll be happily married. Besides, I'll tell them you lost the baby. No big deal."

Gwen felt a growl rising in her throat. Never in her life had she wanted to hit anyone as much as she wanted to hit Gertie at that moment. She knew it was the wrong thing to do, but she just couldn't help herself. She balled up her fist, just like her brothers had taught her, and she punched Gertie right in the eye.

Gertie let out a loud wail, her hand covering her eye. Gwen stood there, knowing people would come to see what the ruckus was about. She planned to tell everyone right there and then that she had done nothing wrong.

When Mr. Blue saw Gwen standing over Gertie who was sprawled in the dirt, he didn't hesitate. He grabbed her by her ear and pulled her home. Her mother and sisters had come out of the church to see what happened and they followed along behind them. Their three brothers would have to represent the family in church that morning.

When they got back to the house, their mother sat them all down in the parlor. "I want to know what on earth is going on with you! All of you!"

Gwen crossed her arms over her chest. "Gertie

admitted that she started the rumors. I know it's not ladylike to hit someone, but sometimes I think that justice is more important than being ladylike."

Mrs. Blue looked at Gwen and shook her head. "I have to disagree, if you're hitting someone on church grounds during Sunday morning service! What were you thinking?"

Mr. Blue glared at his wife. "She's obviously thinking that you're going to let her get away with whatever she does like you always have. You have turned all three girls into little snobs. Gwen runs around with a different man every other week. We heard she was in trouble, and we both believed it! That tells me there's a problem right there. No more. I'm going to find husbands for all three of them."

Gwen jumped out of her chair. She'd always been the most vocal of the three. "I won't do it! You can't make me marry someone I don't want to marry! What are you going to do? Lock me in my room?"

Mr. Blue's face turned red with anger. "That's exactly what I'm going to do. You have been out of control for too long. From now on you will take all of your meals in your room. You may come out to use the water closet, but only if your mother or I accompany you." He grabbed her by her upper arm and dragged her up the stairs to her small room.

Gwen threw herself on her bed and sobbed loudly, knowing her mother would never hold out against her sobs. She never had, and she never would.

Libby and Bonnie sat in the parlor with their mother listening to Gwen's wails. "Mama, you can't really let Papa lock Gwen up until she marries," insisted Libby. "Can you?"

Mrs. Blue shrugged. "I have no control over him. He's my husband. I was taught to honor and obey my parents and my husband. I should have taught you three girls to do the same thing." She shook her head. "I'm afraid I'll have to let your papa do whatever he thinks is right this time."

Libby and Bonnie exchanged a look. "Would it be all right if we went in to talk to her?" Bonnie asked. She had an idea, one that she'd been formulating for a while, and she needed to talk to her sisters about it.

Mrs. Blue eyed her eldest daughter for a moment before shaking her head. "I don't think that's a good idea. I don't trust you girls not to let her out."

"But...you can't think to keep us apart for as long as it takes to plan a wedding! That's ridiculous." Libby couldn't believe her mother would even think of doing such a thing.

Bonnie reached over and squeezed Libby's hand, her way of signaling that she had an idea.

Mrs. Blue sighed. "I don't know what we'll do. I just know I'm not going to fight with my husband about the punishment you girls have been given. I'm done protecting you from him. After today, I'm done helping you at all. You all shamed me today."

Libby shook her head. "No, Mama. Only Gwen shamed you. We were good."

Mrs. Blue was startled by that for a moment. "Oh, you were. It was only Gwen, wasn't it?"

"I think we'll go up to our room now." Bonnie got to her feet and looked at Libby, letting her know without a word that they had some serious talking to do.

Gwen had always had her own room because she was too bossy to share with her sisters. They liked their room more orderly than she did, and her response was always, "Clean up my stuff yourself then." It worked out better for everyone.

As soon as they reached their room, Bonnie closed the door. She got something out of her dresser drawer and sat down on the bed. Once Libby was sitting in front of her, she handed her the letter she'd gotten.

Libby looked down at the letter. "What's this?"

Bonnie shrugged. "Libby, we both know I have no future in Beckham. Next to you and Gwen, I'm the ugly duckling. Goodness, everyone calls me 'Scrawny Bonnie' behind my back, don't pretend they don't. I've never had a single suitor, while you both have had plenty of men interested in you — and I'm the oldest! I'm twenty-three and an old maid."

Libby started to protest but Bonnie interrupted

her. "I've come to terms with it, Libby. But that doesn't mean I don't want to marry. Unlike you and Gwen, though, I don't subscribe to the fantasy that I will only marry for love. A business arrangement would suit me just fine, so I spoke to Elizabeth Miller, the lady who runs the mail order bride agency."

Libby gasped at that. "Did you get a proposal? Are you leaving us?!"

"Read the letter," Bonnie murmured.

Libby read it and looked up and her sister, confused. "But this letter is looking for three women, not one."

Bonnie nodded. "I was going to talk to a couple of other unattached friends my age but... Libby, we need to leave town as soon as possible. Did you see the look in Papa's eyes? He's really going to marry us off, and I suspect it's to that trio of creepy old deacons from church he's been speaking with every Sunday. I couldn't stand that humiliation.

"No! Not them! He wouldn't dare! I'm only eighteen! Mother wouldn't let him."

"Didn't you hear her? She won't protect you and Gwen anymore, Libby. I know that's hard to hear since she's spoiled you two so much, but I can tell you from experience, that when she gives up on you, it's forever."

Libby had a pained look on her face as if she was trying to figure out a puzzle. Bonnie knew to just wait. Sometimes it took her beautiful sister a little bit longer to catch on, but she always did...eventually.

"So instead of marrying those old lechers, we run away to Texas and marry strangers?"

"At least they're young strangers, Libby. We can start completely from scratch without anyone knowing about this ridiculous scandal. Even if Papa doesn't force us to marry his friends, no one else will want us for a very long time, if ever."

Libby gave Bonnie a sly look. "Do we have to take Gwen?"

Bonnie smiled. "She may be annoying, but she's our sister. She probably needs this more than either of us. Let's rescue her from herself, Libby. What do you say?"

After a moment Libby nodded. "Let's make it happen."

- 1 -

North Texas — October, 1888

Bonnie Blue was not normally the fidgety sort but, after ten days of listening to her younger sisters bicker nonstop as a train hurtled them headlong toward an uncertain future, her nerves were frayed. She needed one of her long, quiet walks but the cramped and constantly shaking train car offered little chance for one.

"I just don't understand why you couldn't have brought my cornflower dress," Gwen, her spoiled and utterly beautiful sister, whined. "It matches my eyes so perfectly."

Libby, the youngest of the three and no less pretty, rolled her eyes. "We didn't really have time to carefully select your wardrobe, Gwen. We had to sneak out under the cover of night because of your scandal."

"It wasn't my fault," Gwen insisted. "That horrible Gertie Landry spread all those wicked rumors about me...about us!"

"But you're the reason she spread those rumors, Gwen. If you hadn't kissed her fiancé—"

"He kissed me!" Gwen interrupted, but Libby paid no mind.

"—Gertie wouldn't have told everyone you were..." Libby looked around to make sure no one was eavesdropping. "*With child*, and that Bonnie and I had also kissed the same boy."

Bonnie couldn't sit there anymore. They'd rehashed their sudden and secret departure from their hometown of Beckham, Massachusetts a hundred times already and she didn't want to listen to it all again. Hauling her slight frame from her hard wooden seat and holding on for dear life, she shuffled her way up the jostling car's narrow aisle.

The second-class car they were traveling in was relatively clean, if sparsely decorated, with a small stove in the center. Unfortunately, the smoke from the engine several cars up — not to mention the dozens of exhausted passengers who hadn't seen a basin of fresh water in days — did nothing for the smell in the cabin. Throwing all her weight against the door at the back end of the car, she managed to open it far enough to slip out onto the platform between cars.

If she'd been making this journey just a year or two earlier, she wouldn't have dared to step outside her car. The platform, if you could call it that, would not have been enclosed — it would have had only a flimsy chain on either side to prevent her from falling between cars. She'd read many news articles about passengers being burned by red hot cinders flying back from the steam engine, or even being thrown from the open platform. But passenger trains were quickly adopting the Pullman Car Works enclosed vestibule design, allowing for safe passage.

The odor of the engine's exhaust was no better outside than in, but even in the dark enclosure of the vestibule, the thundering of the wheels on the track was deafening, drowning out every other sound in the world. It was so loud that it quieted her brain nearly as well as a long solitary walk.

Out here, she could think. Out here, she felt almost at peace. Almost.

Nothing would settle her anxiety about becoming a stranger's bride. Even though she'd sought out Elizabeth Miller, the lovely woman who owned the mail order bride agency in Beckham, she still wondered if she was doing the right thing.

After years spent watching every man in town — young and old — fawn over first Gwen and then Libby, but none paying any attention to her at all, she understood down to her toes that her path would be different. Her mother told her as much on her eighteenth birthday.

"Your gift this year, my dear, are domestic lessons from Mrs. Butterfield." She looked pleased as punch and seemed to expect Bonnie to be thrilled with the idea. But more than anything, she was confused. She knew how to cook, clean and sew as well as the next girl. She even could plink out some songs on their old, out-of-tune piano.

"I don't understand, Mama." She remembered blinking in confusion. It was a strange thing to remember so clearly, but it was such a strange situation that every movement stood out. "Not to sound vain, but I'm a far more competent cook than Gwen, and Libby isn't showing much inclination in that direction either."

Libby was only thirteen at the time, but her days were typically spent singing to herself and dancing around empty rooms as if a man were leading her. Or staring out the windows. She did that a lot. Her teacher called her a flibbertigibbet and Bonnie thought the term suited her baby sister perfectly.

"Yes," her mother agreed, "but your sisters have other...*attributes* that will make them desirable wives. Attributes which you sadly lack."

Mama might as well have slapped her in the face and called her ugly. She was humiliated and it took all her willpower not to shed a tear at her mother's hurtful words. But she was determined not to reveal her pain.

As a petite girl with rather plain features, mousy reddish-brown hair, pale skin — except the parts covered by freckles — and no figure to speak of, she'd certainly heard worse growing up with a school full of cruel children. But to hear her own mother essentially call her 'Scrawny Bonnie', too, was almost too much to bear.

She'd always thought she was safe with her family, especially her parents. Now she knew better. Right in that moment, as her mother was prattling away about Mrs. Butterfield's profound skill at homemaking, Bonnie vowed to never let another person get close enough to hurt her. It was another brick in the wall she built to protect herself, since no one else seemed inclined to do so.

She accepted that she was an ugly duckling compared to her two sisters' swan-like beauty. But she had something neither of them did: Wits. Not only was she smarter than her sisters and all their friends, but she was smarter than most of the boys in town, too.

One day, a particularly doltish boy name Chester shouted after her, "Scrawny Bonnie, Scrawny Bonnie, why don't you eat some honey?!"

Ever so slowly, she turned on her heel and looked him in the eye, a sad expression on her face and concern oozing from her words. "Was that supposed to rhyme, Chester? Poor, poor Chester can't rhyme. Can you even *read*?" She gasped as if she just realized the truth of her statement. "Oh, I'm so sorry, Chester! Would you like me to tutor you after school? It wouldn't be seemly for a banker's son to be illiterate, so I'm happy to help you."

Chester's face grew redder and redder as she continued, scanning the faces of the other children on the playground to see if they believed her. It was obvious they did. "I can read! I can!"

Bonnie nodded and smiled, "Of course you can, dear. Please tell your father that I'm available for tutoring, just in case." Then she tipped him a wink and flounced away, the very image of confidence. But inside, another brick was laid.

By the time Libby had turned eighteen, it was obvious that Bonnie would become an old maid if she stayed in Beckham. Her looks combined with her quick wit — and occasionally sharp tongue — had driven every boy her age into the arms of other girls. She'd never even had an older widower show any interest.

So she approached Elizabeth, who had promptly told her about three triplet brothers in Texas. The idea of moving to Texas, far from her family, was appealing. She wouldn't have to compete with her beautiful sisters, for one thing. Of course, she would miss them terribly because, despite everything, she loved them. She would also miss her three handsome brothers, but she rather liked the idea of finally leaving her parents' nest.

She took the letter, intending to talk to two other friends her age who were still unmarried, but before she could, scandal had fallen on their house. Gwen's most bitter rival, Gertie Landry, had spread terrible lies about all three sisters, and everyone in town had believed her.

Honestly, it wasn't a far leap to believe flirtatious Gwen had perhaps gone too far with a boy and suffered the consequences. But to suggest that young Libby and, of all people, Bonnie herself had kissed the very same boy? That should have set off warning bells to anyone hearing the filth spouting from Gertie's mouth. Unfortunately, the good townspeople of Beckham apparently would rather believe the worst, and the family was suddenly embroiled in the scandal of the year.

When Papa threatened to marry off all three to avoid any more talk, Bonnie could tell he wasn't bluffing. Her sisters were used to getting their way, especially Gwen. All she had to do was muster up a few tears and bat her eyelashes at Papa and he would cave. On the rare occasions that didn't work, Mama could always change his mind. But Bonnie knew firsthand what a hard man he could be, and she understood he meant business this time.

It only took a few minutes for her to figure out the men he had in mind for his daughters — three elderly deacons from church who had always made her feel uncomfortable. It was the way they eagerly greeted all the young ladies of the congregation, and the fact they were confirmed bachelors, meaning no women had ever wanted to marry them. Instinctively, she knew that marrying any one of them would lead to a life of misery.

She'd noticed Papa talking with them more frequently of late, and she suspected that he'd originally been trying to find a husband who would be willing to take her. But once this scandal broke, he saw his chance to be rid of all three of them in one fell swoop.

As frustrating as her sisters were, and as much as she hated to live in their shadow, Bonnie could not stand by and watch them married off in such a way to men who clearly did not deserve them. And she refused to be humiliated in such a manner herself. She'd spent her entire life in a constant state of humiliation, she wouldn't willingly enter into an arrangement that could only bring her more of the same.

Their parents had locked Gwen in her room until Papa could find someone willing to marry her, so Bonnie and Libby conspired to get them out of town as soon as possible. While Bonnie reported to Elizabeth that she and her sisters would happily marry the three rancher brothers in Texas, as long as they could leave as soon as possible, Libby squirreled away all the money they had. Train tickets wouldn't be an issue because the prospective grooms paid for those, but they would need traveling money, as well as 'just in case' money.

Libby looked at Bonnie funny the first time she mentioned it. "Just in case what?"

Bonnie smiled at her sweet, silly sister's innocence. "Just in case we decide the ranchers are worse than the old, lecherous deacons, of course."

Libby gasped at the very notion, but immediately set out to scrape together anything she could — without stealing, of course. She also packed a single trunk with the most basic necessities for all three of them. Three trunks and piles of missing clothes would have been noticed, most likely by their nosey brother Hank, but they were using a single trunk that had been tucked in the corner of their room for years. It was all but invisible.

For a moment, Bonnie considered enlisting their brothers for help in escaping, but she quickly discarded the idea. Benedict was too busy helping Papa at the mercantile and, even though she was a year older than him, she knew he'd side with their parents. Hank would help, if only to get under Ben's skin, but he wouldn't be able to stop himself from crowing to Ben. And Percy...well, Perfect Percy would tattle because there was nothing he loved more than to follow the rules. No, the boys would have to find out about their defection at the same time their parents did — *after* the train pulled out of the station.

The days dragged by as they waited for the ranchers' reply. Gwen was only allowed out of her room to use the watercloset, and neither Bonnie nor Libby could get near her. But they didn't try very hard — just enough to seem believable to their parents.

All the while, Bonnie was watching and planning. She couldn't risk sneaking into Gwen's room until moments before they left the house for good. Judging by Gwen's miserable expression every time Mama escorted her to the W.C., she would readily agree to running away.

But would she agree to marrying a stranger? Considering Gwen's spoiled and willful nature, Bonnie was doubtful, so she worked up a story that they were going to visit an old friend who now lived in Wiggieville, Texas. As much as she hated to lie to Gwen, it was the only way to be sure she would get on the train. If she learned the truth, she might refuse out of spite, and then the entire plan would be ruined. They'd be forced to marry the old men.

When Papa came in one Sunday afternoon smiling

from ear to ear, Bonnie knew their time was growing short. "Deacons Smith, Bellafonte and Jackson have agreed to marry you girls," he announced at the dinner table. "It took some sweet talking and the promise of a few favors, but they finally agreed."

Libby paled and Bonnie worried her sister might faint dead away right there in the mashed potatoes. But a not-so-gentle kick to the girl's shin brought a flush to her cheeks. "Oh-oh, th-thank you, Papa," she managed to choke out before hiding her horror behind her glass of water.

"Yes, thank you for watching out for us, Papa," Bonnie added, much more convincingly. "While I wouldn't say this episode has been a blessing, exactly, it has at least brought with it a blessing. I will finally have my chance to become a married woman. What a relief!"

She beamed at her father who, at first, looked slightly puzzled, then broke into a grin. "That's my smart girl! You know I'm only trying to do what's best for you and your sisters. Now if only Gwen understood that."

"She'll come around, Papa," Bonnie soothed.

But the sound of Gwen's screams and then wails kept the entire house awake most of that night. She cried for two days straight, refusing all meals and resorting to using a chamber pot rather than showing her face outside her room. Her fast broke on the third day, but she remained hidden in her room, forcing their mother to empty her pot.

Papa wanted the weddings to happen immediately, but Bonnie convinced him that it would be unseemly if they didn't wait at least a month. "By then, it will be obvious that Gwen is not...in a family way. It will appear to be a more joyful occasion, don't you think?"

Papa's brows knit together in thought, but eventually he nodded his big bushy head. "Good thinking, Bonnie. You've got a good head on your shoulders. Mr. Jackson will be well-pleased with his new wife, even if he picked the short straw."

Bonnie blinked. "Short straw?"

Papa flushed red. "Uh, nothing," he stammered as he hurried from the room. "I'll set everything up for a month from today."

Whatever guilt she'd been feeling about lying to her parents and potentially embarrassing the old deacons vanished. They'd drawn straws to see who would end up stuck with her! They deserved whatever humiliation they got.

A week before the wedding, Bonnie dropped into Elizabeth's office at her home, as she had every day for two weeks. "Oh, Bonnie! I just received the brothers' response. Here."

Bonnie carefully took the sealed envelope Elizabeth held out and sank into a nearby chair. It was from the oldest brother, Walton, proposing marriages between the three brothers and the three sisters. There was little else except the funds for three second-class train tickets.

Almost before she finished reading, Bonnie was rushing down to the station to buy tickets for the next train out of Beckham, which was bright and early the next morning. Only then did she return to Elizabeth's to dash off a reply with their arrival date.

She could hardly contain her excitement at the dinner table that night. Libby looked at her funny several times but Bonnie didn't want her sister acting strange in front of the family so she didn't tell her until after they'd retired for bed. When she finally did, Libby squealed like a little girl who got a doll at Christmas.

"Shhhhh!" Bonnie laughed, covering her sister's mouth with her hand. Only after Libby regained control of herself did Bonnie let go.

"Tonight's the night, Libby. Are we packed?"

Libby was flushed and breathless. "Yes! All except our toiletries. I did pack some for Gwen. Mama's old set was in a trunk in the attic. Do you think God considers that stealing, Bonnie?"

"I don't think so, Libby. Not under the circumstances. After all, we'll be leaving Gwen's set, which is far nicer, if Mama ever needs a spare set."

Libby looked mollified, then quickly jumped to their traveling trunk and pulled out a small bag. "I managed to collect twelve dollars," she said proudly.

Indeed, that was probably the most money her little sister had ever seen, but it would make for thin eating for three people all the way to Texas. And no 'just in case' money.

"Good job, Libby. Now let's get changed into our traveling clothes and wait for the house to go to sleep."

In the wee hours of the morning, Libby and Bonnie dragged the trunk out of the house using a small carpet as a sort of sled. Much to Bonnie's surprise, they hardly made a sound. Of course it was more difficult when they made it outside. They had to carry the heavy trunk to the barn where they kept the horses and a small buckboard wagon.

They'd just dropped it for the third time when someone stepped out from behind a tree. "And where do you think you're going?"

Libby squealed again but slapped both hands over her mouth before waking the entire town. The figure stepped out into the moonlight. It was their brother Hank.

"Hank!" Bonnie hissed. "What are you doing out here?"

Hank smiled easily and leaned back against the tree, crossing his arms across his broad chest. "You first, big sister."

Bonnie was grateful he couldn't see her blush. She paused for a moment, wondering what to do, but decided there was nothing for it. She'd have to trust him.

"We're running away, Hank. We've received proposals from ranchers in Texas and we're leaving on the first train. We're taking Gwen with us."

She squared her shoulders, daring her younger brother to argue. He didn't argue, but he did look concerned. "You're leaving without saying goodbye? You know that'll kill Mama."

Bonnie thought bitterly that their mother would only be sad over losing Gwen and Libby, but instead said, "Probably so, but they haven't left us any choice. You can't honestly think we should marry those vile men Papa picked out for us, can you?"

Something like anger flashed across Hank's face. "No! Absolutely not. I tried to talk him out of it but you know how he gets."

All three stood on the front lawn just looking at each other for a few moments. Then Hank stepped forward and grabbed one of the trunk's handles. "Looks like you need a little help."

Bonnie turned the key as slowly as she could to keep the tumblers inside the lock from making a racket. The screech of the hinges pierced the silence of the darkened house and she expected to hear her father come rumbling down the hall at any moment.

Pausing, she heard nothing but his muffled snores.

Once the door was fully open, the three siblings were shocked. The room itself was a mess. Clothes littered every surface and, as her eyes adjusted, Bonnie could see that many of the dresses were torn or cut to shreds. The chamber pot stood in a corner, thankfully not too full, but the smell from it almost gagged her.

But there was something else, another scent she couldn't quite place. When she caught sight of a sleeping Gwen she knew what it was: hopelessness.

Gwen had always taken great pride in her appearance, but after being held captive in her room for two months, and then told she must marry against her will, she'd given up on herself. Her normally perfect blond curls had matted into a flat, greasy helmet. Her porcelain skin was speckled with blemishes. And, judging from the sharp stink coming off her in waves, she hadn't bathed properly since being banished to her room.

Libby looked wide-eyed at Bonnie, the question left unasked. What were they going to do? The train would be leaving in four hours, and there was no way they could board with Gwen looking like death warmed over. There was only one option.

"Quick," Bonnie whispered. "Hank, get her coat. Libby, find a traveling dress and anything else to make her presentable."

As the other two rushed to their tasks, Bonnie

knelt beside her sister and gently shook her shoulder. "Gwenny, wake up. Gwen, can you hear me?"

"Muh?" Gwen mumbled. Bonnie grimaced at her breath. It smelled worse than the chamber pot.

"Gwen, do you want to marry old man Bellafonte?"

Gwen's eyes snapped open, filled with fear. "No!" she cried out.

"Shhh! You can't make any noise, understand? If you don't want marry him, we need to leave tonight."

Gwen rubbed the sleep from her eyes. "But where will we go?"

"To visit my old school friend, Anna Simpson, in Texas. We already have tickets and we've packed as much as we dare because no one in the family knows. If we wake them up, they'll stop us and we'll be forced to marry those old men."

Just then Hank hurried in with the coat. Gwen gasped and scrambled backward. "No!" she whispered, tears filling her eyes.

"Darling, Hank is helping us," Bonnie whispered. "He's the only one, and he's promised to keep our secret until his death." She turned to give her brother a withering look. "Which will come quickly if he betrays us."

Of all her siblings, Hank was her favorite, but the look she gave him told him exactly what kind of pain he would suffer if he ever said a word. To his credit, he nodded somberly and wrapped the coat around

Gwen's trembling shoulders.

"Let's go, Gwenny."

"But...look at me," she whined quietly. Bonnie was cheered that some of her vanity was returning. That seemed like a good sign.

"I have a plan, but we have to leave now."

Thirty minutes later, the three sisters were on the front porch of Elizabeth Miller's home. The house was dark and Bonnie hated to wake Elizabeth but they were desperate so she pounded with all her might.

She'd sent Hank on to the station to drop off their trunk and return the buckboard back home. They could walk to the station in just a few minutes. Saying goodbye to him had been harder than she imagined and she was suddenly grateful they were sneaking away in the night.

After the third hard pounding on the door, a candle flickered through a window when the draperies were pulled back. Elizabeth's white face peered out.

"Ladies, come in," she gushed when she opened the door. "What's the trouble? Oh!" She'd finally gotten a good look at Gwen, who was utterly embarrassed.

"Our train leaves in about three hours, Elizabeth," Bonnie explained. "We need your help."

The kind woman nodded and proceeded to scurry around the house. Two hours later, Gwen looked almost like her normal beautiful self. Her hair was clean and dressed, as was her body, and she smelled faintly of lilac. It was an amazing transformation, and it had a profound effect on Gwen.

"Libby, why didn't you bring my cornflower dress," she whined as she spun around in circles. The pale yellow dress matched her hair perfectly and left everyone in the room breathless by her beauty.

Libby rolled her eyes. "I see you're back to normal again," she muttered.

"What was that?"

"I said—"

"We need to let Elizabeth get back to sleep and get ourselves to the train before it leaves us to a horrible fate," Bonnie interrupted, trying to stave off what would undoubtedly turn into yet another bickering match between the two.

The pair glared at each other but finally nodded, gathering up everything they brought. Elizabeth gave Bonnie a hug and showed them out. As they were hurrying down the path to the street, relief washed over Bonnie that Gwen hadn't recognized Elizabeth as a matchmaker and that Elizabeth hadn't spilled the beans.

Then Elizabeth called after them. "Now you three have a safe journey, and be sure to write to tell me how everything is going with those three brothers!"

Bonnie raised a hand in acknowledgement but kept the other two moving.

"Brothers? What brothers?" Gwen asked.

"Our brothers, silly," Bonnie replied. "Now get moving or we'll miss the train." She cast a sideways glance at Libby, who was biting her bottom lip to keep from laughing. In the distance, a lone whistle sounded.

Bonnie was startled out of her reverie by a conductor opening the door of the car and stepping out. He was as surprised to see her as she was him.

"Oh! Miss, I apologize, but you should return to your seat soon. We're approaching the next stop and it's dangerous to be out here when the train is stopping."

"I will in just a moment. Thank you, sir."

He nodded curtly and entered her car. As the door closed, she heard his clear, ringing voice announce, "Weatherford Station! Next stop Weatherford Station!"

Bonnie's stomach clenched and apprehension wormed it's way through her. This was their stop. Their long journey was over. There would be three men standing on the platform, waiting to whisk them off to the closest pastor or judge. And then their new lives would begin.

She wondered if they would draw straws.

=2=

The gentle rustle of yellowing leaves pulled Bart Dalton out of a deep slumber. Lazily peeking one eye open against a brightening sky, he was mesmerized by the swaying of the branches overhead. He couldn't think of a better way to start the day.

A blue mockingbird landed on a branch, causing two leaves to begin a slow, fluttering descent toward the ground. On the branch, they were kept apart, barely brushing against one another, but once they left their straight and narrow home, they seemed to take joy in dancing with each other on the light morning zephyrs.

A strange heaviness settled deep in his chest. Hunger maybe? Something — a speck of dust perhaps — must have blown into his open eye because it started watering something fierce. Wiping away the wetness, he took a deep breath and threw back the wool horse blanket he used when he was on one of his 'safaris'. It was time to pack up camp and head back.

As soon as he joined his brothers to start a ranching 'empire' — his brother Walton had grand plans — Bart made it very clear that he would need to take off into the wilds of north Texas from time to time to keep his itchy feet from getting too itchy. Nearly every month since arriving, he'd disappeared to go 'hunting' for a few days, though he often never even bothered to unpack his Winchester.

Ever since he left his family's Oregon City home when he was seventeen, Bart had been a drifter, and he liked it that way. He was only there to help his brothers get up and running, then he'd be back on the trail, searching for something he suspected he'd never find — mainly because he didn't know what 'it' was.

He had to admit, he'd grown fond of their little parcel of land. Parcels, really. Walton had claimed his own stretch. He'd written them each — Bart was in San Francisco and Nate was in Colorado — to come claim their own parcels, and they'd dropped whatever they were doing to help the oldest of the triplets.

The moment they arrived, the brothers got busy building cabins for each of them, one after the other. Bart's had been the last, and it was definitely the sparsest. That didn't bother him, though, because when he wasn't at Walt or Nate's place, he was out on safari.

He discovered the term the previous year after reading H. Rider Haggard's *King Solomon's Mines*. It was a grand adventure tale set in the heart of Africa, detailing Allan Quatermain's search for a missing man. Bart immediately related to the lead character and decided to dub his little jaunts 'safaris'.

His brothers didn't really understand his need to keep moving. Walton was more than ready to settle down and have a family — he said as much in his letter inviting the brothers to join him — and Nate was getting close, even though he didn't like to admit it.

"What's the hurry," Nate would say whenever Walt brought up the topic of wives. "We're only twenty-seven, brother. Let's get the ranch established, then we can have our pick of ladies."

Yet Nate had taken great pains to make sure his cabin was furnished with the finest furniture and frilliest things he could afford. Any time Bart gave him guff about it, he'd turn beet red. "Easier to get all this stuff now than to have to do it all over again later," he'd mumble. Meaning, when he got married.

Bart had less refined needs. He built himself a small bed out of scrap wood and used a few clean blankets as a mattress. He'd slept on harder surfaces most of his adult life, and he didn't want to get spoiled by one that was too luxurious. Too many of his traveling buddies had been tempted by the superficial comforts of a home life, and he didn't want to join their ranks.

On paper, his cabin looked identical to his brothers', but step across the threshold and it was a whole different story. Walt had ordered three stoves for them, which went to waste at Bart's place. He'd never lit it, not once. He did manage to cobble together a small table and one chair, for the odd days he was there, but he mostly used it when he sat down to pull on his boots before heading to Walt or Nate's for mealtime. There was no other furniture, and certainly no decorations, in the cabin. And it was about as much home as he ever wanted to have.

Stretching deeply, Bart gathered up his bedroll and kicked dirt on the smoldering embers of last night's campfire. With all the dead leaves blowing around, he didn't want a wildfire to kick up. He strapped everything on his horse Roamer's saddle and gave the chestnut pony a good rub down.

Roamer had been his constant companion for most of his life. Growing up on a dairy farm in Oregon City, the triplets were tasked with caring for the farm's animals, including the handful of horses they had. One dark morning, when the boys were about ten, they stumbled out to the barn to start their chores and found one of their pregnant mares on her side, thrashing around in agony.

Nate ran back to the house to get Pa, while Bart

ran to the business end of the horse to see what was wrong. The colt's head and forelegs were hanging out of poor Dimple but nothing more was coming. She was breathing hard and fast, trying to stand up and push, but the colt wouldn't budge. Finally, her eyes rolled back and she laid still.

Bart worried that she'd fainted, or worse, died. He was also worried the colt would die since Dimple stopped pushing. Running on instinct, he reached out and tore open the white sac covering the colt's face. Grabbing the legs as he'd seen Pa do a few times, he started tugging. The colt didn't move. He tugged harder, putting all of his meager weight into it, and got some traction.

Only when Walt wrapped his arms around Bart's waist and lent his bulk to the effort did the colt slide easily from Dimple and plop to the ground. A shiny dark face looked up at Bart, blinking in confusion. As he was cleaning it off, his father rushed in.

"What the Sam Hill..."

Walt was soothing Dimple, who had come around but was still exhausted. "Bart saved them, Pa! Dimple here stopped pushing so he grabbed the colt and pulled it right out!"

Pa crouched down next to where Bart was rubbing the colt with an old blanket. It was small, smaller than any he'd ever seen, and was barely moving.

"How long was he stuck, son?"

"I dunno, Pa. Dimple was in a bad way when we got here and he was half poking out of her. Do you think he's gonna be okay?"

"Only God knows for sure, but you did a fine job of giving him a fighting chance. I'm proud of you, Bart."

Bart stroked the poor, exhausted colt's head, wondering how such a tiny critter could worm its way into his heart so quickly. *Please, God, let this one live. I'll take care of him, I swear!* He wasn't much for praying — he and his brothers mostly pinched each other during church — so he hoped God heard this one.

Pa patted his shoulder, then turned to his brothers. "I'm proud of all of you for working together to save this mare and her baby. When you three team up, there's nothing that can stop you."

Of course, the colt not only survived, but thrived. It was touch and go for a while, but between Dimple and Bart, Roamer grew stronger and bigger than any runt should have. Almost from his birth, he followed Bart wherever he would go. They had a connection his brothers envied. They even tried to fool Roamer into believing they were Bart but the horse was smarter than they were.

When it came time for Bart to leave Oregon City at the tender age of seventeen, his family didn't think twice about letting him take Roamer. The horse wouldn't allow anyone else to ride him anyway, so there was no point in keeping them apart.

As Bart finished up Roamer's morning rub-down, he noticed an inch-long split in one of the horse's hooves. "Dang," he whispered. Roamer whinnied back at him, wondering what his person was upset about.

The split was still small, and didn't go very deep, but it would still take a few months for it to grow out. Roamer could be ridden for short rides, but nothing like he was used to. Bart would have to tend to it to immediately to make sure the crack didn't expand. That would be painful for Roamer and could cause an infection.

Saddling up, Bart patted his old pal's neck. "We'll take it slow and then I'll get you all fixed up. By the time that hoof has grown out, maybe the ranch will be stable enough that we can get back out on the trail again. How does that sound, boy?"

Roamer grunted and set off for home.

"Aw, fiddlesticks," Bart cried when they were about halfway back to the ranch. He'd promised Walt to meet him and Nate at the train station today at three o'clock to meet some cattle buyer or another. Bart hardly paid attention to the business part of their concern, preferring to focus on the physical part of the job.

"Go on your safari, Bart," Walt had said, "but

promise on Roamer's life that you'll be at the station. Promise."

"Yeah, yeah, big brother," he vaguely remembered saying. "I won't let you down."

If he'd remembered his promise before setting off for home, he would have been early, but as it was, they'd gone a fair clip out of their way. Judging by where the sun was in the sky, he was going to be late. Of course, his brothers would expect that, but they would also expect he'd show up eventually. He just hoped the cattle buyer fellow didn't get too riled up.

Bart smiled as he rode Roamer at a slow amble through the bustling town of Weatherford. It was three hours north of the ranch and was the closest train stop.

Though the Dalton brothers spent most of their time in Wiggieville, which was just an hour from them, they'd had occasion to visit Weatherford quite a bit, mainly to pick up bulk supplies they couldn't get in much smaller Wiggieville.

As he passed the Weatherford Church, he tipped his hat at the preacher out front cutting sunflowers from a small garden. From the big basketful he had, it looked like he was collecting them for some event.

"Afternoon, Reverend."

The preacher looked surprised for a moment,

confused even, before replying, "Mr. Dalton."

Bart was taken aback for a moment. How did the man know who he was? He'd never been to this church. Walt had dragged him and Nate to the Wiggieville Church several times, but never in Weatherford.

Walt! He'd been here for some time before his brothers arrived. No doubt people in town knew him. Rather than correct the preacher, he just nodded and kept Roamer moving, not wanting to further irritate his undoubtedly irritated brothers.

"Aren't you supposed to be at the station, Mr. Dalton?" How did he know their business? Well, it was a small town and word spread fast. Walt probably stopped in to say hello or something.

"On my way there now, Reverend."

"See you soon," the reverend called after him cheerfully. Bart waved a hand noncommittally behind him. He had no intention of making a three-hour-long trip to go to church. His little safari had cost him three days of work already, which he'd have to catch up on before he went socializing again.

As he drew closer to the train depot, Bart recognized his brothers' wagons. "Shoot!" he murmured. Walt specifically asked him to bring his, too, because they were expecting some freight or another on the train, along with the cattle buyer. He'd plumb forgot. Even if he hadn't, going all the way back to the ranch and getting it rigged would have made him really late instead of just thirty minutes or so. He could only hope that whatever Walt ordered would fit in the two wagons.

The town's small depot was a muted yellow with brown trim, and didn't have much room inside for resting. Consequently several people were sitting outside in the shade of the building — three ladies and four men, one of whom was pacing furiously on the platform looking each direction down Main. Even from a distance, he could tell it was Walton. He'd always been pretty tightly wound.

Bart brought Roamer to a stop near the platform, doing his best to ignore the glare Walt was burning into his back as he tied the horse to a post and dusted himself off. What was he so fired up about? After twenty-seven years, he should know by now that Bart was late as often as he wasn't. Maybe more so. Couldn't the two of them entertain a solitary cattle buyer on their own for a few minutes?

Climbing the slightly warped steps to the platform, he couldn't help noticing the extreme beauty of two of the three ladies seated on a long bench. One was yellow-haired with a dress that matched, the other was a brown-haired girl whose innocence could take a man's breath away. The third woman, who sat a little ways from the others, was pleasant enough to look at but the sour expression on her face made him feel sorry for whatever man put it there.

She was a tiny little thing with the fairest skin he could ever remember laying eyes on. There was a fetching smattering of freckles across the bridge of her pert nose, and her brown hair — no, wait, it was more chestnut than brown — complemented her coloring nicely. But when she flashed her brilliant green eyes at him, the hair on the back of his neck stood on end.

Why on earth was she glaring at him?

Walt rushed up and grabbed him by the arm, turning him away from the fearsome little spitfire. "Where have you been?" Walt hissed under his breath. "We've been waiting for half an hour!"

"So? Why didn't you just take the man to the saloon and wait for me there?"

Bart looked over at the two other men on the platform, but they were engrossed in their own conversation and heading down the stairs. Nate was standing a few paces away, staring off into the distance. Every few seconds, his eyes would cut over to the pretty brunette and then over to his brothers and back to the distance again. He looked in shock.

"What's going on, Walt? Where's the cattle man? And what the heck is wrong with Nate? He looks like he just got hit in the face with a frying pan."

Walt flushed and dropped his gaze. Clearing his throat, he said, "Well, he did, after a fashion."

Bart was keenly aware that the fiery redhead was watching his every move. He was flattered but also a bit puzzled. There were two other identical versions of him standing right there — why was she watching him?

Walt pulled him toward the bench full of ladies and stopped in front of the spitfire. "Miss Bonnie Blue, this is my brother Bart Dalton."

Miss Blue pursed her lips and stood, squaring her shoulders before thrusting her delicate right hand at him. His massive paw practically swallowed it as he shook it as gently as he could manage. He was afraid of breaking her, despite the fiery daggers she was shooting at him with those dazzling green eyes.

"Bart," his brother continued, "meet your bride."

-3-

"You're late." It was the only thing Bonnie could think to say to 'her' groom. But he was only hers by default. And that was assuming he didn't turn around and walk away.

It probably shouldn't have surprised her that the eldest Dalton — Walton, of all names — had been as deceitful to his brothers as she and Libby had been to their sister. But she was surprised.

The moment she and her sisters stepped off the train, she spotted two men who looked identical. The odds of there being a set of twins *and* a set of triplets meeting that particular train seemed low, so she assumed the third brother was simply out of sight.

Raising a tentative hand to the men, Bonnie started across the platform with Libby and a clueless Gwen, who was prattling on about the stagecoach ride they were supposed to be taking into Wiggieville to see Anna. The men met them halfway.

"Are you ladies the Blue sisters?" asked one of the men.

"Who are you?" Gwen said, as rude as ever.

"I'm Walton Dalton, and I pick you," replied the man. Then he did the most amazing thing. He pulled Gwen into a kiss — right there on the platform in front of God and everyone!

Gwen took care of him, though, by stomping on his foot, but he didn't seem deterred. In fact, he seemed more determined than ever, going so far as to say the preacher was standing by. And poor Gwen had no idea what was going on.

"Mr. Dalton," Bonnie said, addressing Walton and trying to keep the panic from her voice, "I'm Bonnie. I'm the oldest sister." He seemed completely nonplussed by this news so she elaborated further. "I believe I'm the one you're supposed to marry."

"I don't care who's oldest," he said, gazing down at Gwen. "I'm marrying this one."

He might just as well have punched Bonnie in the stomach. She'd come all this way expecting to marry the eldest brother and who had he gone for? Gwen, of course. She shouldn't have been surprised, really, but it still stung.

"I believe your letter said there would be three of you," she managed to squeak out.

"That's my brother Nate," Walton said, nodding at his brother before flicking his eyes around the platform. "Bart should be here by now but I'm sure he'll be along."

Bonnie didn't really care about the inconsiderate brother Bart, who couldn't be bothered to keep an appointment. She had higher expectations from her future husband.

She turned to look at Nate but he couldn't seem to rip his gaze away from Libby, who was blushing furiously and peeking up at him from behind her dark lashes. This wouldn't do at all. She refused to be the consolation prize for the one who didn't show up on time.

"Libby's the youngest!" she fairly shouted, drawing surprised looks from everyone. Surely he would do the right thing and choose Bonnie over her baby sister. But of course Nate had been just as surprised as Gwen at the situation he'd found himself in, and he simply looked confused.

To his credit, he adapted much more quickly than Gwen did, as soon as Walton explained, but Bonnie once again found herself ignored and rejected in favor of her prettier sisters. Bitterness settled over her heart at the realization her life would be no different outside of Beckham.

The next twenty or so minutes went by in a blur of explanations and recriminations. Bonnie hardly heard any of it, she was so hurt and humiliated. She'd traveled for what seemed like an eternity in hopes that life in Texas would be different, that she'd have a chance to find love. Of course, she would never admit that to anyone but it was her heart's secret desire.

And now...now she was leftovers. The discarded garbage the other two brothers didn't want. She was table scraps! It was all she could do to choke back the tears as they waited for the tardy youngest brother.

She knew he'd be handsome because his brothers were. It was impossible to tell them apart by sight yet but it was easy to figure out just by checking to see which of her sisters one or the other was ogling.

Regardless, his looks hardly mattered because, no matter how she turned it over in her mind, he was going to be disappointed that he was stuck with her. He didn't know it yet, but he'd drawn the short straw.

What had she been thinking, bringing her sisters along? She'd registered with Elizabeth's mail order bride agency to leave Beckham — including her family — behind. With nothing to compare her to, her future husband might have been pleased with her. She was extremely skilled at homemaking and, when not standing next to her beautiful sisters, she wasn't altogether homely.

She'd ruined her entire life by putting the welfare of her sisters ahead of her own, just as she'd always done. Never once growing up had they shown her the same courtesy, so why did she feel so responsible for them? They certainly didn't refuse the advances of Walt and Nate, even though Bonnie made it very clear she expected to be the first chosen.

For five full minutes, she sat on that bench and hated her sisters. She wished and prayed for a runaway train to jump the tracks and barrel across the platform, taking them all with it. She would be the lone survivor, and the only person to turn up at the group funeral. Of course, she would be draped in black but, behind her dark veil, she would be smiling. Maybe even laughing.

Then Libby reached over and squeezed her hand. The poor child was trembling. Bonnie's frozen heart melted, and she gave her youngest sister an encouraging smile. She couldn't begrudge either sister happiness, nor would she wish misery on them. And marrying those lecherous old deacons would have been a life sentence of misery.

Well, if she couldn't have love, she would at least do everything in her power to make sure her sisters were happy and cared for. If these two men, who were so entranced by their beauty, didn't do right by them, they'd have Bonnie to answer to.

As for her, she had no choice but to accept the errant Dalton as her husband. What little money they had left after the train journey wouldn't be enough for her to buy a meal, much less a ticket back home. The question was, would he accept her?

It looked like she was about to find out. Walton was striding across the platform to meet with a third man who looked just like him. Well, not *just* like him, she realized. There were subtle differences between them.

Walt was thicker and stouter, while Bart was lean. His jawline was a little more angular than either brother and he had a mop of unruly black hair that badly needed cutting. The stubble on his chin hinted that he hadn't seen a razor in several days, and his clothes were in desperate need of washing. Even his poor old horse was filthy. She could only imagine what he smelled like — the man, not the horse.

As late as Bart was meeting them, Bonnie would have thought he'd have a little giddy-up in his get-along, but in fact he seemed quite unperturbed. Clearly the man was unreliable, inconsiderate and untrustworthy.

Wonderful.

Bonnie was just thinking that maybe marrying Deacon Smith would have been preferable to a layabout ne'er-do-well when Walt led his brother over to make introductions. Swallowing her pride — what was left of it, anyway — she stood and did her best to not glare at the man. Alienating him before he even found out they were to be married wouldn't help matters.

It wasn't lost on her that she could have a sharp

tongue so she focused on taming it for the time being. She practiced in her head all the pretty things she should say, all compliments and flirting. After watching Gwen do it for so many years, some of it had to have rubbed off on the ugly sister.

But the moment Bart's deeply tanned and calloused hand enveloped hers, the second his rich brown eyes met her own, all the words — every word she'd ever learned — flew right out of her head. A strange drumming roared in her ears, and she was surprised to discover it was her heart beating wildly. The palm he was holding so gently in his strong hand was suddenly wet with perspiration. Bonnie had never been left speechless in her life, and she didn't understand her strange reaction to this man.

But the spell was broken when Walt introduced her as Bart's bride. The look of sheer horror that flashed across his face was enough to bring her out of her stupor. Her brain was still trying to play catch-up but two words managed to rise to the surface. Two words that would show she was no one to be trifled with. Two words that would perfectly signify her disdain for him.

"You're late."

–4–

art barely heard her admonishment because the word 'bride' was still echoing in his brain. Bride? What bride? He didn't have a bride.

Flicking a questioning glance at Walt, who was grinning like the devil he was, Bart suddenly understood what was happening. Ever since his brothers answered his call for help, Walt had been nagging them to take wives. "They'll take care of the homesteads while we're out working," he'd say. "A wife is just as important to a rancher as a good cowboy. It's the next step in building our empire, brothers."

The half-stunned, half-smitten look on Nate's face told Bart everything he needed to know. It didn't take a banker to put two and two together — or in this case, three and three. Walt had gone behind his and Nate's backs to send away for some eastern brides.

Well, he wasn't having any of it. He'd told Walt and Nate on that very first day that he would only be staying long enough to help get the ranch running smoothly, a year at most. He wasn't about to get saddled with a wife he didn't want. Besides, it wouldn't be fair to her when he finally left.

With a start, Bart realized he was still holding the tiny spitfire's delicate hand. It felt soft and warm in his own big paw, and for some reason he didn't fully understand, he was loathe to release it. Before he even had a chance, she snatched it away and thrust her fists to her hips, nearly setting him on fire with her glare.

"I understand this comes as a surprise to you, Mr. Dalton," she said, her voice filtering through the noise in his head. "It must be a bitter disappointment to you that you're stuck with me, but I suppose that's what happens when you're late for appointments."

Disappointed? What was she talking about? He wasn't disappointed as much as he was stunned and angry at Walt. And what did she mean 'stuck' with her? Did she really think he was going to marry a total stranger?

Walt jolted him out of his stupor with a sharp slap to his back. "Ready to head to the church?"

The church? The church! That's why the preacher had said those things. That's why he was collecting flowers! Oh, lordy. This wasn't going to be pretty.

"Um, Walt..."

"Um nothing," interrupted his overbearing, bullheaded brother. "We can't keep the good reverend waiting. Let's go!"

Finally, Bart's anger got the better of him. "I'm not going anywhere, Walt. No offense to this lovely young lady, but I told you I didn't want a wife. I told you I was leaving here in a year or so. Did you think you could bully me into marrying, just like you've bullied me into doing stuff all my life? No more, brother. It stops now. I'm not gonna marry...what's your name again, miss?"

Her face had softened some, though he didn't know why. "Bonnie Blue," she nearly whispered.

"I'm not gonna marry Bonnie Blue here, only to leave her in the lurch when it's time for me to go. What kind of man would do that? Not this man, that's for darned tootin'!"

Walt's smile turned hard and he pulled his brother off to the side. "What do you think you'll be doing if you leave her standing here on this platform, brother? 'Sides, look at her. It's not like she's got a lot of prospects."

Bart looked over at Bonnie, but he didn't understand what his brother was talking about. What was wrong with her? Sure, she was just a little bit of a thing, but that was nothing some hard work and good food couldn't cure.

Didn't matter. He wasn't about to let himself be

roped into marrying anyone, especially out of guilt. Walt brought her out here under false pretenses, so she was his responsibility, not Bart's.

"Mr. Dalton," she called. "May I have a word in private?"

Bart didn't like the gleam in her eye, and he really didn't like the way his heart beat just a little faster when she said his name. But he couldn't very well not talk to her. He'd just explain the situation and send her back home — and make Walt pay for her ticket.

When they were away from the other two couples, she turned to face him. "Mr. Dalton—" she started.

"You can call me Bart," he interrupted. "Listen, I'm sorry about my brother, and I'm sorry about all of this—"

It was her turn to interrupt. "Please stop and listen to my proposition."

Her tone was firm but not commanding. Seeing as how he was going to be putting her on the next train back to wherever she came from, the least he could do was listen to what she had to say.

"Thank you," she said when he waved a hand at her to continue. "This...this hasn't turned out like I expected at all. I can only imagine how you're feeling about it. But let me propose an...arrangement."

She moved toward him a half a step, her skirts rustling and brushing the leg of his trousers. He was amused by the fact that the top of her chestnut head just barely reached his chin. She had to crane her neck back just to look him in the eye.

Glancing over her shoulder to make sure no one could hear them, she lowered her voice and continued. "I want only the best for my sisters, which was why I deceived Gwen about our real reason for coming here. I suspect the same holds true for your brother Walton."

She was right, of course. As riled as he was, Bart wouldn't hold a grudge because his 'big brother' was doing what he thought was was for the best. Even though it wasn't.

"I hatched this plan to escape from a...bad situation back home. It was my idea, I planned it, I risked everything to come here, and now I'm about to be left in the lurch with no option open to me but to return home and endure a life of misery."

Bart felt bad for the little fireball. He had a hard time believing she'd stand for any sort of mistreatment, so whatever she was facing must be wretched indeed.

"From what I gather, you have no desire to settle down, is that right?"

"That's right. I'm a bit of a drifter, y'see. Always have been. I'm only here to help my brothers, and then I'll light out again for wherever the trail takes me. It's no life for a lady, and I'm not one of those scoundrels who would take advantage of a situation like this."

He hoped he was making his meaning clear because

he didn't want to offend her delicate sensibilities by speaking more plainly. But she seemed smart as a whip and proved it by nodding.

"I appreciate that. So what if I suggested a plan that benefitted us both?"

He was intrigued. "I'm listening."

She cut her eyes around them again to make sure the coast was clear. "You don't want a wife, but you probably do need someone to manage your homestead. When you finally leave for good, do you expect your brothers and their wives — my sisters — to add your homestead to their list of duties? That seems a bit unfair doesn't it?"

Bart had honestly never thought of what would happen to his homestead after he left. He was more focused on getting the ranch up and running. "I suppose..."

"I have never had any romantic delusions that I would marry for love, but I can assure you that I would make an excellent wife, even if in name only. I was the best cook in my hometown, so I would keep you well fed while you're here. I can sew faster than any professional seamstress, so I can make and mend all your clothes. And, as you might have noticed, I'm smart. I can keep your books so you'll never have to think about such things."

Those were all things he hated doing, that much was true. But he still wasn't sure what she was suggesting. The confusion must have been written all over his face.

"My proposition is this: We marry today as planned."

His eyes popped wide and his jaw dropped as he tried to find the words to balk at her. But she continued quickly, before he could object.

"I will make a wonderful home for you to return to every night, full of food and comfort. That's probably something you didn't see much of during your travels. In return, I won't have to go home. I will live a life of independence, managing your portion of the ranch for you when you leave. If you ever decide to come back, everything will be in order for you. Think of it as your home base from which you can travel to your heart's content."

Bart was surprised at how appealing the idea sounded to him. Good meals were few and far between on the trail, much less a comfortable place to lay his head. And it would certainly ease his brothers' burden to know at least his portion of the spread was cared for when he left.

"So you'd basically be my house manager?" He'd been around enough to see that rich folk had all sorts of funny jobs for people, such as the lady in New Orleans who had a house manager.

Bonnie was familiar with the term and smiled. "Exactly."

Bart scratched at the scruff on his chin absentmindedly as he thought things over. "Miss Blue—"

"Bonnie, please."

"Alrighty. Bonnie. You have to know that I light off every now again as it is. Can't stand being all cooped up like a chicken. Also, my place...it's not made for a lady such as yourself. I'm afraid you'll be mighty disappointed when you see it."

The smile she gave him didn't quite reach her pretty green eyes. "Trust me, the alternative is far worse. Do we have a deal?"

Bart looked over at his brothers, his heart aching with happiness that they seemed so taken with their brides. It would worry them if they knew about this bargain, and he didn't want them to worry. He'd tell them when the time came to leave, just as he had when they were seventeen.

"Under one condition," he finally replied. "You and I will know it's a business partnership, not a real marriage. But everyone else needs to believe we're happy or it will lead to too many questions. Agreed?"

Bonnie thought on this for a brief moment before nodding her head and sticking her hand out for him to shake. That seemed overly formal under the circumstances, and now was as good a time as any to start the charade.

Grabbing her by the shoulders, he pulled her into

his chest, wrapping his arms around her tiny frame in a brief hug. Her hair smelled of train smoke and roses, and before he knew what he was doing, he'd buried his nose in her neck and was breathing deeply.

Behind him, he heard Walt whoop in approval. He was already buying their act.

Too bad Bart hadn't been acting.

=5=

Bonnie reeled when Bart finally released her from the hug. Luckily, he draped his arm over her shoulder as part of the performance he was giving for his brothers, otherwise she might have toppled over right there on the platform.

Never in her life had a man embraced her in that way, never mind one as handsome as Bart, and it sent an unfamiliar sensation through her. Quite honestly, it made her uncomfortable. She could only hope he would keep those kinds of embraces to a minimum in the future. And if he didn't, she'd have to put her foot down.

The next couple of hours were a whirlwind as the six of them walked down to a small, quaint church. They all stood in a line in front of the preacher and he married them at the same time. The only thing she really remembered from the quick ceremony was being embarrassed at how filthy she was and, of course, the kiss.

"You may now kiss the brides," the preacher said, smiling at them expectantly.

Bonnie blinked up at Bart, wondering if his kiss would warm her as much as his hug had. Her cheeks flushed as he dipped his head and barely brushed his lips across hers. He smelled of sandalwood and campfire, and the scruff of his beard felt scratchy. It was over in a heartbeat but she knew her lips would burn for hours. She'd never been kissed before, after all. It had to be natural to feel that way after a first kiss.

No wonder Gwen likes to kiss men so much, she thought as Bart led her back down the aisle.

But the moment they all stepped outside, the slightly dizzy feeling she had was replaced with cold, hard reality.

"Bonnie Blue, you'll have to ride with one of my brothers," Bart said, rather nonchalantly for someone who was trying to keep up appearances. "I didn't bring a wagon and I don't think you'd be comfortable riding with me on Roamer for three hours."

"You can ride with us," chimed in Libby, giddily holding onto Nate's arm and grinning from ear to ear. Nate didn't seem totally thrilled with the idea, but Walt was already dragging Gwen off to his wagon so he didn't have much choice.

She rather expected Bart to follow them, but as soon as he helped her into the dirty bed of Nate's wagon, he'd hopped on his beautiful horse and set off out of town on his own. Bonnie knew it was foolish to feel hurt but she couldn't stop herself.

For three hours, Bonnie's bones were rattled in the back of the Nate's buckboard while she listened to Libby prattle on like a schoolgirl. Dust swirled around the back of the wagon and settled on her, which seemed just about right after everything that had happened.

For three hours, she stewed on the events of the day. From expecting to be the first bride chosen to being the one nobody wanted. It shouldn't have surprised her, but it did. She'd let her guard down, forgot her place in the world. She wouldn't make that mistake again.

For three hours, she relived the brief hug and light kiss Bart had given her over and over, trying to burn every detail into her memory. Even though she knew they weren't real, those were almost certainly the only embraces she would ever enjoy for the rest of her life, and she didn't want them to fade from her memory.

And she couldn't forget the moment he called her lovely. No one had ever said that about her before. Undoubtedly he'd simply said it to be kind, but she couldn't deny that she liked it.

Dark fell before they reached the Daltons' cabins. They were all clustered within walking distance and, as far as Bonnie could see in the moonlight, they were nearly identical. Smaller than she expected, considering their husbands were ranchers, but they could always be expanded.

Nate pulled to a stop in front of one cabin. "This is Bart's...I mean, your home, Miss Blue."

Bonnie liked Nate immediately. He was kind and had good manners. Not like their ringleader, Walt, in the slightest.

"I suppose I'm Mrs. Walton now, Nate, but I'd prefer if you called me Bonnie."

He helped her down from the wagon, both of them looking around for Bart, who should have been there to offload his new wife. "Should I bring the trunk inside, Miss...um, Bonnie?"

The sisters had agreed to have her sort out their belongings, which would undoubtedly need ironing, at the very least. "Please and thank you, Nate."

She grabbed one end of the trunk and together they lugged it up the steps to the front door. Unsure of whether she should knock or just walk in, she paused. But Bart saved her from making the wrong choice by throwing the door open wide and beaming at them.

That smile. It did things to her insides. So much so that she had to look away to catch her breath.

"Welcome home, Bonnie Blue. Here, let me grab

THE DRIFTER'S MAIL-ORDER BRIDE

that."

He and Nate set the trunk inside the front door, and Nate beat feet out of the house. She couldn't blame him for wanting to spend some time alone with his new bride. Hopefully their mother had taught poor Libby everything she needed to know for her wedding night.

Bonnie winced at the irony. She was probably the only Blue sister who knew what went on in the marriage bed, and she was the only one who wouldn't be making use of that knowledge.

Ever.

Taking a deep breath, she took a good look at her new home. The main room was tiny — not much bigger than her and Libby's bedroom in Beckham — but it probably looked bigger than his brothers' homes because he had no furniture. None!

There was one pathetic little rough hewn table along a wall and one chair. Just one! Where on earth would they both sit? A few short steps took her to the sad excuse for a kitchen. The only thing going for it was a brand new stove but, as far as she could tell, there were no utensils, pots or pans, and she suspected she wouldn't find any plates or cutlery, either.

Dismay must have been written all over her face because Bart stuttered an apology. "I'm real sorry, Miss...I mean, Bonnie. I only use this place to sleep in, and sometimes not even then. I eat all my meals at

Nate's or Walt's, and I never entertain."

"I see," she mumbled.

"But listen. I ran ahead and raided Walt's place a little. I wasn't sure what you might need to get started, but it's all in that crate there."

"You stole from your own brother?" What kind of man did she marry? By all indications, Bart had seemed to be a respectful man, even if he was perpetually late. But now she was worried he was a thief — or worse.

He smirked at her as he started pulling pans and jars from the crate. "You ask me, he deserved it for playing Nate and me like suckers."

He had a point. After all, Walt hadn't given his brothers time to prepare for a wife, so she could hardly blame Bart for not having a beautifully furnished house with a fully stocked larder. Besides, Gwen would most certainly not miss any of the supplies Bart was setting on the rough board that acted as a shelf. Poor girl never learned to cook.

Looking over what he'd snitched from his brother's place, Bonnie quickly planned out a meal. It wouldn't be fancy but it would be filling. She was starving, and Bart looked like he needed a few good meals to put some meat on his bones.

Leveling a firm gaze at him, she used her sternest tone. "You understand that *this*—" she waved a hand around the small cabin, "—isn't acceptable long-term, right? Obviously, this house requires more furnishings, as well as such silly things as food."

Bonnie was disarmed by the twinkle in his eye. Normally that tone made people fidget at best, and cry at worst. But Bart seemed almost amused by it.

"Understood, ma'am," he said with a wink. "Make a list and, when I get a free day, I'll take you and your sisters to Wiggieville for the bigger stuff. Till then, I'm afraid you're gonna to have to rough it a little."

"I'm not afraid of that," she said, shooing him out of the kitchen. "First off, let's get something in our bellies. All I've had to eat today was a piece of your brother Nate's jerky."

"And what's second off?" he asked, settling himself at the table.

"We talk."

–6–

Bart had ridden poor old Roamer home as hard as he dared but it was still half the speed the horse was used to. He tugged at his reins, urging his master to let him fly, like the good old days, but Bart was concerned about that split hoof. A lifetime of traveling had taken a toll on the old boy, a toll Bart was just now noticing.

The three-hour ride back to the ranch after his hasty wedding gave him time to think. What had Walt been thinking? Of course Bonnie had been right that his brother sent away for those three women with only the best intentions, but Bart was mighty sick of Walt making decisions like that for him. Maybe Nate didn't mind, but he wouldn't stand much more of it.

The worst part was putting him in such an awkward position. That poor woman thought she was getting a new husband, a new life. No matter what Walt was expecting, Bart refused to mislead her. But she barely batted an eye at his plain talk, and then she'd come up with a plan that, at first blush, sounded pretty good all around.

Bonnie was the smartest of those three sisters, that much was certain. Probably the smartest woman he'd ever met, and he'd met quite a few bright sparks in his travels. On top of that, she had integrity, which was a rare quality in most human beings, in his experience.

As a drifter, Bart was distrustful by nature. If you didn't watch out for yourself, someone was bound to come along and take advantage. He'd had hidden pockets sewn into all his traveling clothes for the sole purpose of hiding valuables, and he had to use all his fingers and toes to count how many times they'd served him well.

But for some strange reason, he wasn't at all suspicious of Bonnie. It might have been different with her sisters — that blonde was trouble if he ever saw it and the quiet brunette was too naive to trust — but Bonnie was as true a woman as he'd ever met. He couldn't explain how he knew in such a short time but he did.

Which made him all the more glad he didn't try to deceive her. She wasn't under any illusions that theirs would be a 'real' marriage. He'd get a house manager and she'd have a home. Basically, she'd be his most trusted employee.

Perfect!

The more he chewed on it, the more he liked the arrangement. He'd have the freedom to do as he pleased, and she'd feed him. Now that Walt and Nate had new brides — real ones — they would probably be far less keen on him dropping in for meals. And, while he could cook a mean campfire tater, real meals were beyond his abilities.

Riding along, he thought about his cabin. For the first time, he was ashamed of how bare it was. He didn't know Bonnie very well, but he knew she deserved better than an empty shell of a home. He didn't even have any food in the house. Well, a quick stop at Walt's place would remedy that!

As slow as he had to go to protect Roamer's hoof, he knew the wagons wouldn't be too far behind him. He had barely enough time to lug the crate full of dry goods into the cabin before he heard a wagon pulling up. He didn't even have time to light the stove, not that he'd know how to do it.

He was impressed by Bonnie's acceptance of his hovel and amused by her businesslike manner about it all. She was absolutely right to expect better accommodations, and he'd let her decorate the place however she liked. She'd be the only one living there most of the time anyway, so he couldn't care less.

While Bonnie worked some kind of delicious smelling magic in the kitchen, he set about scrounging up some wool horse blankets from the barn. While he was out there, he checked on Roamer and found him favoring the foot with the split hoof. Not too much, but Bart decided he'd let the old fella rest up for a few days before riding him again. Good thing they had other horses to choose from.

As he laid the blankets in front of the fireplace, he couldn't help noticing Bonnie watching him. The way her emerald gaze followed his every move warmed him, perhaps a little too much for a 'strictly business' relationship. He needed to break the spell.

"There ya go," he announced, spinning on the heel of his boot and waving a hand over the thin pallet. He almost laughed at her confusion. "You said you weren't afraid of roughing it. Well, till we can get you your own bed, this'll have to do."

His glee at teasing her almost erupted as laughter so he turned away and sat down in the house's lone chair with his back turned to her. "And I hope you don't mind standing up to eat till we can scrounge up another chair."

Trying desperately not to snicker, he waited for her to berate him or throw a fit, but all he heard behind him was a deep sigh. Turning to look at her, his teasing grin slipped away. She was standing with her back to him and her shoulders were shaking, but she wasn't making a noise. His shoulders had been shaking too, but he was trying not to laugh. From the slumped look of her, he was sure she was trying not to cry.

Shame wasn't something Bart was used to feeling, but it filled him with horror now. He'd been joking around with her but it only took a moment for him to see it from her point of view. She was exhausted after a long journey, hungry, in a new place and situation, and now she had to sleep on some ratty old blankets on the floor.

He felt like a total heel.

Leaping up from his seat, he went to her and spun her around. The way her head was bowed in defeat nearly broke his heart. "I was just joshing you a little, Bonnie Blue. I swear. Don't cry."

When he pulled her into his arms, he thought it would be awkward, but it wasn't. She fit perfectly into the nook of his shoulder, and her warmth and softness felt like home. Her head settled against his chest, where his heart was suddenly hammering away like crazy.

"Shh," he whispered, smoothing her thick chestnut hair. "I was planning to sleep on the floor the whole time. You can have my bed, of course, but I warn you, it ain't much better than that pallet."

They stood there swaying for a moment — or an

THE DRIFTER'S MAIL-ORDER BRIDE

hour, Bart sort of lost track of time — before she pulled back, sniffling. "I'm so sorry, Mr. Dalton—"

"Bart," he choked out, his voice strangely hoarse.

She nodded. "Bart. I don't know what came over me." Her voice was shaky and she trembled under his hands.

If they'd been in a dancehall, he would have guessed she was smitten with him but as it was, he knew she was just tired. So was he, now that he thought on it. All he wanted to do was eat and get some shut eye. Maybe the morning would bring more clarity to this strange arrangement.

"You go sit down, and I'll dish up whatever this is you rustled up for us," he instructed. She started to object but he just pointed at the table. "It's the least I can do after making my pretty new wife cry on our wedding night."

Something flashed across her face but disappeared as soon as he tipped her a wink and a grin. She gave him a small smile and settled herself at the tiny table. He really did need to do something about that.

The sausage and sauerkraut that she'd whipped up out of almost nothing smelled like heaven. He already knew it would be the best meal he'd had in months — his brothers were better cooks than him, but not by much — and he couldn't wait to dig in.

Settling the now-empty crate from Walt's on the other side of the table, Bart sat and raised his cup of water, tapping against Bonnie's. "To a long and happy partnership."

= 7 =

onnie still felt foolish for crying in front of Bart. She'd never cried in front of her sisters, much less total strangers. She'd just been so overwhelmed with everything that had happened that it all came spilling out when he said she'd be sleeping on the floor. That was not how she'd always envisioned her wedding night.

But this wasn't a real marriage, she reminded herself. It was a business arrangement — a partnership, just like he'd said in his toast at dinner. If she didn't keep her silly schoolgirl expectations in check, she would be in for a lifetime of sadness.

As it turned out, dinner was quite nice. Bart was charming and funny, and she truly liked him. He regaled her with tales of his travels, including one story about how he and Roamer managed to outrun a pack of hungry wolves in the wilds of Montana. It was quite thrilling!

"Do wolves normally try to attack such big animals as a horse and rider?" she asked as she cleared the table.

Bart sprawled across the small square of wood, resting his head in one hand as his gaze clouded over with memories. "Ha! That's nothing. I've seen a pack take down a bull elk with no trouble at all, and those rascals can get feisty. We were small pickin's to them."

"How did you manage to escape?" Bonnie found herself almost breathless wanting to know the details. Bart was a good storyteller, that much was certain.

"It was all Roamer. Those wolves were nipping at his fetlocks and I was trying to aim my shotgun at 'em when ol' Roamer managed to kick the leader right in the snout. I don't know how he did it without breaking stride but all I heard was a loud yip and the biggest of the bunch went tumbling and rolling off. I saw a splatter of blood on the snow behind us so I know he took a heckuva blow."

"This was in winter?!" Bonnie was shocked.

Bart laughed at her expression. "Sure. I don't just amble about in the summer, y'know. When my feet start itchin', they don't care what the temperature is outside."

They fell into a comfortable silence as Bonnie cleaned up the supper dishes. For the first time since

THE DRIFTER'S MAIL-ORDER BRIDE

she stepped off the train, she was happy things had turned out the way they had, even if it wasn't exactly how she imagined.

Walton had been too overbearing for her taste and she was sure they would have had a contentious marriage had he chosen her. Nate seemed quite nice, but perhaps a little too solicitous. Bart, on the other hand, was very engaging. There was no pressure on either of them to perform as a spouse would, so they were already comfortable with each other. This might work out well after all.

Just as she was drying the last dish, a knock sounded on the door. Glancing over to the table, she saw Bart sprawled across it snoring softly, his head resting on his arm. She couldn't stop from smiling. He looked like a little boy who'd played too hard.

Opening the door, she found one of Bart's brothers, but she didn't know which one. She was almost certain it was Walton — she marveled at his ridiculous name once again — because of his clothes, but it was rather dark out so she decided to play it safe.

"What can I do for you, Mr. Dalton?"

He must have been used to being confused for his brothers because he quickly identified himself as Walt and asked to speak with her. Not wanting to wake Bart, she pulled her shawl from a bent nail next to the door — she'd have to find a better solution for that as well — and stepped outside.

"It's kind of a delicate subject," her new brother-in-law mumbled, shuffling his feet and not meeting her eyes. After the day she'd had, and how rudely he'd rejected her, she didn't have a lot of patience with the man.

"Just say it," she sighed. "I'm tired and would like to go to sleep."

He took a deep breath and spat it out. "Does Gertie have any idea what happens in the marriage bed?"

Gertie? Gertie Landry? How did he know the woman who spread lies about them all over Beckham, and why would he care what she knew about the marriage bed? And why would he ask Bonnie?

Wait just a minute... She had a sneaking suspicion she knew exactly who he was talking about but she couldn't resist humiliating him a little.

"Who's Gertie?" she asked innocently.

His eyes grew wide and if there'd been anymore light out on the porch — if you could even call it a porch, it was so small — she would have been able to see exactly how red he turned. "Isn't that my new wife's name?"

She was torn between amusement and irritation. A small, resentful part of her thought it was awfully funny that spoiled Gwen's new husband couldn't be bothered to remember her name. But a bigger part of her felt protective of her sister, no matter how irritating she could be.

"No," she said with as much steel as she could muster, "it's not. Her name is Gwen. Maybe you were the right man to marry my sister after all." Of course, she was really thinking *I'm so glad you didn't pick me.*

Bonnie had always assumed their mother'd had the same talk with her sisters as she'd had with her, but according to Walt, Gwen was clueless. She couldn't fathom why their mother wouldn't have talked to Gwen and Libby. Of course it was a very short discussion, with not much information, but the tutor Mother had hired to teach Bonnie homemaking also included some very frank — and rather embarrassing — talks about how she could please her future husband.

Sadly, she'd never get a chance to use her knowledge, but the least she could do was help her sister have a happy home life. Especially after she deceived her so dreadfully. But she couldn't resist taking one more pot shot at Walton.

"After you, Mr. Dalton. I'm afraid I don't know which of these pitiful shacks is yours."

Gwen had been taking a bath as Bonnie talked to her about the facts of life and marriage. She did her best to impress upon her spoiled sister that she was a married woman now, and she had certain obligations. She didn't want to scare the poor thing, but she also didn't want her to be too surprised. Of course, having never been intimate with a man, Bonnie had no practical knowledge, but she trusted that Mrs. Butterfield had been honest about the act of lovemaking.

On the short walk back to Bart's home — *her* home — all she could think about was how clean her arms felt after helping Gwen wash her hair. What she wouldn't give for a bath tonight. Her bones ached with exhaustion but a bath...it sounded heavenly.

Walt kindly escorted her home and before he went back to his place, she asked where their well was. He pointed in a general direction and scurried away, no doubt anxious to find out how much Gwen had learned.

Stepping into the house, she found Bart where she'd left him, snoring like crazy. Not wanting to disturb him, she quietly took the oil lamp from the table and went in search of fresh water. As tired as she was, a bath would be the perfect way to start her new life. A clean slate and a clean body.

Gwen had told her how time consuming it had been to fill that small tin tub with water but Bonnie didn't care if it took all night. She would rest as the water heated, and then sleep like a baby for the rest of the night.

It took a couple hours to find everything she needed. Out back was a tub exactly like Gwen's, which Bonnie dragged into the cabin's sole bedroom. She tried to be quiet so as not to wake Bart but he slept like the dead. It didn't take long for her to stop being so considerate and just go about her business.

Bucket after bucket, she lugged the water into the house and transferred it to the tub when it was hot. The thought of resting while the water heated was appealing but she was pretty sure she wouldn't wake up till morning if she dared close her eyes, so instead she started cleaning.

The house was barren but it had a layer of grime so thick there was no way she could get it all in a single pass. She focused on the kitchen because the one little oil lamp Bart had — another item added to her mental to-do list — shed just enough light in there to see well. Well enough, anyway.

By the time the bath was full and hot, Bonnie had managed to thoroughly scour every inch, including the floor. That was one chore she could scratch off her list for the next day, and that felt good.

It wasn't until she started undressing that she realized the tiny bedroom didn't have a door. At least Gwen's new bedroom had a curtain. Yet another thing to add to the list. It was already so long, she was afraid she wouldn't remember it all come morning.

No matter. Bart was fast asleep at the table, and he'd already told her she could have the bedroom. She wasn't entirely comfortable undressing so close to a strange man, but she wasn't about to let all her hard work — and all that clean, hot water — go to waste.

The process of undressing was made more difficult thanks to her aching muscles, but she finally freed herself from her last stitch of clothing and eased herself into the water.

"Mmmm..." she moaned. A simple thing like a bath — something she'd taken for granted back home in Beckham — felt like heaven on earth, even if the tub was small and cramped. Her muscles practically sighed with relief as they loosened in the heat of the bath.

Only once every inch of her, including her hair, was clean, did she allow herself to lean back and soak. The thought of soaking in more than a week's worth of filth normally would revolt her but her sore muscles won that argument. Before she knew it, she was drifting in and out of a warm slumber.

"Jumping Jehoshaphat!"

Bonnie screamed in response to the man's voice, and had just enough of her wits about her to hunker deeper into the tub. Bart was standing in the doorway, eyes bulging and mouth gaping as she tried to cover herself with the tiny scrap of rag she'd been using as a washcloth.

"Get out!" she screeched.

He blinked twice before flushing a deep crimson. Covering his eyes, he spun on his heel and hurried out of the room.

"I'm so sorry, Bonnie!" he called from the other room. "I was half asleep and forgot you were even here! I-I-I...I think I'll go for a walk and let you finish in private."

Bonnie waited until she heard the front door slam before releasing the breath she'd been holding. It came out as half a sob.

She wasn't sure how long she'd been dozing, and she had no idea how long Bart had been looking at her, or even how much of her body he'd seen. All she knew was that, for some unfathomable reason, his hasty retreat made her want to cry.

Bart barely slept that night.

After accidentally walking in on Bonnie taking a bath, he ran out of the house like he was on fire. He made a beeline for the barn, grabbed a brush and started furiously working on Roamer. He'd already brushed him once, but the horse didn't seem to mind the attention.

What must she think of him, catching him staring at her like that? He hadn't meant to, but he'd never seen anything quite so beautiful in his life, and it took all the effort he could muster to look away.

She'd been slouched so low in the bath that her dark red hair was tumbling in lovely waves over the back of the tub. One arm dangled over the side, water slowly dripping from one limp, wrinkled finger, and her smooth knees were poking out of the cloudy water. The oil lamp cast a warm glow over the scene, and Bart knew it would be etched in his mind until the day he died.

He wanted to tell her that he hadn't seen anything more of her, that her modesty was intact — or as intact as it could be, under the circumstances — but that might embarrass her even more. The last thing he wanted was for her to feel uncomfortable — or, heaven forbid, afraid. He'd rather gotten used to the idea of a house manager, and he honestly enjoyed her company. He'd hate to see her leave.

Nope, the best thing would be to keep his mouth shut and pretend nothing happened.

He made busy work for himself in the barn for a good hour to give her time to do whatever it was she needed to do, then snuck back in as quietly as he could. The lamp in the bedroom was out, so he settled himself on his makeshift pallet.

But sleep didn't come until late, and then it was light and troubled. He felt like he'd barely been asleep five minutes when one of Nate's blasted roosters started to crow. It was going to be a long day.

His eyelids felt dryer than the Texas desert as he pried them open, but his nose perked up instantly. The smell of brewed coffee and frying bacon woke him up quicker than a bucket of water could.

He hadn't so much as taken off his shirt before he hit the sack, so all he had to do was roll up his pallet, just as he'd do if he was out on safari. Tossing it into a corner casually, he said, "Something smells mighty good."

Bonnie peeked around the stove and smiled. Something seemed a touch off about it but it was probably leftover emotions from the night before. "You need a little fattening up, Mr. Dalton, so it's a good thing you got stuck with me as a...wife. My sisters are hopeless in the kitchen."

There was that word 'stuck' again. Who in their right mind would think a man could ever be 'stuck' with her as a wife? If he'd been the marrying kind, he'd be tickled pink to have such a comely, talented and smart woman as Bonnie. As it was, he was tickled to have her as his house manager, which was about as close to a wife as he ever wanted to have.

He also couldn't help noticing she was back to calling him Mr. Dalton again. That stung a bit. He didn't know which to address first so he kept his mouth shut and hoped the whole thing would blow over.

As he and his brothers worked in silence on building a new fence that morning, Bart's thoughts kept returning to Bonnie. Of course the vision of her in the bathtub kept flashing unbidden into his mind, but more than that, he marveled at her ability to adapt.

THE DRIFTER'S MAIL-ORDER BRIDE

She was a tough woman who didn't mind hard work.

What little time he'd spent with her sisters made him glad his brothers had picked first. Neither one of those gals would have had the sense to see the situation for what it was and offer a solution. The blonde one would have probably thrown a tantrum and that other...well, she was like a lost puppy.

In fact, over breakfast, Bonnie had very efficiently laid out her plans for his spread — their spread. She would scope out a prime spot for a garden that morning, before going to teach her sisters how to cook. She'd come back and scrub the rest of what she called a "shack" and start working on a list of furnishings to buy or order.

"I hope that's not too forward of me," she said, peeking at him over the rim of the chipped enamel of her coffee mug.

He'd barely said a word because he was too busy stuffing his face with the most delicious breakfast he'd eaten in months, years maybe. It was just simple bacon and eggs, stolen from Walt's pantry, but the eggs were cooked perfectly. Just soft enough for the yolks to run a little so he could dunk his crispy bacon in it.

Walt always burned eggs. Of course, Bart never complained. He'd spent far too many mornings on the trail hankering for any kind of food, so burnt was fine by him. But Bonnie's cooking...he could tell by the two meals she'd already whipped up — out of thin air, it seemed — he was going to be back to his fighting weight before Roamer had time to heal.

"Mr. Dalton? Did you hear me?"

Bart shook himself back to the present. Setting his fork down with a clink, he gave her a stern look. "I got plenty of money to buy whatever you need but I won't let you buy a single thing till you start calling me Bart. I ain't Mr. Dalton; that's my Pa!"

A light blush pinked her pale skin as she dropped her eyes and smiled. "Well…"

"What wife calls her husband by his surname?" he continued, breaking into a grin. "Heck, we don't want anyone to suspect this ain't a real marriage."

Her lips went from a sweet smile to a grim line. What had he said? She glanced up and nodded curtly, hopping up to clear the dishes.

"Quite right, Bart. I hadn't thought of it that way."

Where they'd had a pleasant, easy conversation over breakfast, the silence between them now was tense. She didn't seem angry, but something had changed. Worst of all, he suspected it was something he'd said but, as he twisted the wire of the new fence in place, he couldn't for the life of him figure what.

It made his feet itch.

-9-

Bonnie loved her sisters — she truly did — but she couldn't help being frustrated at having to teach them how to boil water. Why had Mama not taught her two beauties at least a few basic skills?

It didn't matter now. She would have to be the one to teach her sisters how to keep a home, even though it meant she had less time to dedicate to setting up her own household.

But it wasn't all bad. She'd already talked with her brothers-in-law in private and made arrangements for compensation. Until Bart could take the new brides into Wiggieville for provisions, she could raid their stores, including Nate's henhouse. Considering how bare Bart's pantry was, this seemed more than fair to her.

Spending the morning with her sisters was

refreshing. That was strange because they'd spent their entire lives trying to spend time *away* from each other, but out here in the vastness of Texas, they all were eager to see each other.

Gwen fairly glowed when she opened the door. There was a bounce in her step and a certain maturity Bonnie had never seen in her before. She smiled inwardly that their little talk the night before had produced good results. It was a minor miracle that Gwen hadn't run screaming down the streets of Weatherford the moment she heard what was in store for her, but to be so happy in just twenty-four hours? It made Bonnie's heart swell with happiness and pride for her once-spoiled sister.

Libby, on the other hand, seemed rather glum for a new bride. That was strange because she'd been so excited to get married, and Nate seemed like such a considerate and patient man. When she announced that she'd made her poor groom sleep on the floor, Bonnie stifled a giggle because hers had done the same.

She didn't dare tell her sisters of her arrangement with Bart because they'd probably laugh at her. Either that or get worried, and she didn't want that either. Honestly, she was perfectly happy with their business partnership. It was all she ever expected out of a marriage anyway. Better, in fact, because neither of them had any expectation of love or romance. All that brought was heartbreak and too many mouths to feed.

She just needed to stay on top of her feelings because this morning over breakfast, she'd let her guard down the tiniest bit and Bart had quickly reminded her of her place. Their marriage wasn't "real" and she had no claim to his heart. Whatever schoolgirl fantasy she'd had on the trip to Texas, this was her reality. All she had to do was remember that.

"Hoo boy, somethin' smells mighty good!"

Bart came tromping through the front door, his filthy boots scattering chunks of dirt everywhere. He tossed his dusty hat at the bent nail where she'd hung her shawl, no doubt dirtying the precious heirloom knit by her grandmother.

"Boots!" she cried, tending the gravy she planned to pour over some leftover biscuits Gwen had given her. "And could you please leave them and the hat outside?"

He stopped dead in his tracks, a perplexed look on his face, before doing as she asked...and grumbling the whole time. By the time he came back in, she was setting a steaming plate of biscuits and sausage gravy on the table for him. He immediately forgot his irritation at having to live like a civilized human being.

"Ain't you gonna eat with me?" he said, settling himself on the old crate and pushing out the chair with his toe.

"I really have quite a lot of work to catch up on," she protested. "I spent all morning teaching my sisters how to make bread so I haven't had time to take care of this place."

"One thing I learned on the road was to never skip a meal if'n I could help it." One eyebrow shot up and he looked at her like a teacher would a student. She couldn't help but laugh and dish herself up a plate of food.

"Where'd you find all this grub anyway?" he asked through a mouthful after she'd sat down across from him.

"I took your lead and raided your brothers' pantries," she said slyly. She rather liked feeling naughty, even though she'd had permission to take the food. Bart didn't need to know that.

Now both eyebrows shot up. "You don't say... I may have misjudged you, Bonnie Blue."

"No doubt about," she sniffed.

He chuckled in response and kept eating. From beneath her lashes, Bonnie watched him chew. She liked the angle of his jaw, and the tumble of his brown hair. He was so different from his brothers that she wondered how they could be triplets. Bart was by far the most handsome of the three, and that was a fact.

"Why did you go?"

"Hmm?" He was still chewing.

"When you were seventeen. Why did you leave

home?"

Bart was silent for a minute before answering. "Still don't rightly know. I just know I had to go. Alone. Been alone ever since."

This shocked Bonnie. "You mean you never see people? Ever?"

He laughed good-naturedly. "Naw, I travel with folks here and there. Sometimes I stop for a spell to earn some money. But I try not to go to the same place twice, and the men I travel with are drifters like me. You don't get too close to those kind of men."

That sounded more reasonable. Appealing, even. "Tell me more," she pleaded. He was such a good storyteller.

Wiping his sleeve across his mouth, he grinned at her. "Okay, why not? Let's see... There was the time I accidentally insulted a Lakota chief in the Dakota Territory and had to outrun him and a bunch of his warriors. Phew, that one was close! After I realized what I done, though, I couldn't blame him much."

Bonnie was on the edge of her seat. "What did you say to him to make him so mad?"

Bart cleared his throat and turned red. "Well...I... uh...I got mixed up on my Sioux words — you know Lakota are Sioux, right? Anyway, I thought I was giving the chief's daughter a compliment, but I mixed up 'pretty as a butterfly' and 'stupid as a butter churn'."

Bonnie burst out laughing. It would be hard to

blame any father for defending his daughter against such an insult. She made a mental note to learn the local Indian language before trying to compliment anyone.

"What about you, Bonnie Blue? Tell me one of your favorite adventures." A gleam sparkled in his eyes as he leaned back against the wall and relaxed.

"I don't have any," she shrugged. "I grew up the daughter of a well-to-do merchant. I'm the oldest and he was bitterly disappointed that I wasn't a son. My brother Benedict came next, so he was happy but I don't think he ever really liked me all that much, especially after Gwen came along."

A little crease formed at Bart's brow. "Why?"

Bonnie laughed, hoping he didn't catch the slight hint of bitterness in it. "Haven't you seen her? She's 'Gorgeous Gwen'! All the boys in town groveled at her feet, including Papa. I was just 'Scrawny Bonnie'."

That brought a full frown to his face. She tried to pretend it meant nothing to her, that she was above the cruel nickname, but he must have caught her tone.

"What a bunch of horse puckey! No wonder that girl's so spoiled." He broke into a grin. "Hoo boy, is Walt gonna have his hands full with that one!"

Bonnie tried not to snicker, but couldn't help herself. He was right. Gwen was spoiled and had absolutely no homemaking skills. Walton was in for some meager meals until she could learn to cook.

"Speak of the devil, Walt's probably ready to head back to work by now. I best skedaddle."

He jumped up from the crate and hustled to the door, but just before he stepped out, he turned back to her with a smile. "That was the nicest lunch I've had in I don't know how long. I thank ya, Bonnie Blue."

The funny warm feeling in her tummy lasted the rest of the day.

-10-

The next few days went by much the same as the first. Bart would wake up to delicious and amazing smells wafting out of the kitchen and, after some energizing banter with Bonnie, he'd head out deep into their land with his brothers. They'd return for lunch and, by dinnertime, they were all tuckered out.

By the way Walt whistled every morning, Bart suspected things were going relatively well with his new wife, at least in the bedroom. Sure, there was the odd afternoon when he came back from lunch on the grumpy side, but Walt would never complain to his brothers about his marriage. It would show weakness.

Nate had always been the quiet one of the three, and it was no different now. Bart could tell something was troubling his brother, but he didn't share and Bart wasn't about to ask. If either of them wanted to talk, he'd be there. Just as they'd be there for him. Not that he needed to talk.

Nope, things were chugging along just fine with Bonnie. After a long day of work, he spent one evening building a door for her room. It was the least he could do after walking in on her during that bath, the memory of which still tickled his brain at the worst possible moments.

She loved to hear stories from his travels and he never realized how much he enjoyed telling them. He didn't even have to exaggerate most of his tales, and it wasn't until the telling that he realized how adventurous he'd been for the last decade.

One day he came home for lunch a little early only to find Bonnie stirring a pot of stew absentmindedly while reading *King Solomon's Mines*, one of the only books he ever kept. "How do you like it?" he asked when they settled down to eat.

"It's quite entertaining," she said, but there was a hesitation in her tone.

"But?"

"But...it's fiction. I much prefer hearing the stories of your, what do you call them? Safaris? Even if some of the details are a little embellished." She gave him a knowing smile that made him laugh out loud.

"You caught me! But they aren't all fish tales."

"Maybe you should write a book," she suggested. He'd never really thought of it till now, but his stories were every bit as exciting as ol' Allan Quatermain's. Well...nearly.

"Naw, I don't sit still long enough to even try such a thing. 'Sides, my spelling's right awful."

He grabbed the last hunk of bread on the cutting board and sopped up the last drops of his soup. Hoo boy, she knew how to cook. He'd already had to move to the next notch on his belt and it'd only been a few days.

Bart quickly got used to leaving his work boots and dusty old hat on the porch when he came inside. He'd never been one for housekeeping, but even he could see how much work Bonnie put into cleaning the cabin. It was the least he could do to not track in half their ranch with him every day.

When he walked through the door in his stocking feet that night, the scent of roasting meat hit him hard in the gut. He sure would miss these meals when he lit off for good, so he'd enjoy them while he could. He'd also enjoy the company of a fine woman. Probably the finest he'd ever met.

Not only was she the best cook he'd ever run across, but she was smart, funny and generous to boot. A part of him felt guilty for locking her into a marriage of convenience because she deserved so much more.

She deserved a husband who would appreciate her in every way a man should.

Another part of him was glad his brothers had been so short-sighted when choosing their mates. They'd only gone for outward beauty, and it was true that their wives were conventionally pretty. But Bonnie had a hidden beauty that glowed like the sun when she let you take a peek at it. The other sisters couldn't compare to his Bonnie Blue.

"I don't suppose the mercantile will be open in Wiggieville tomorrow when we go to church, will it?" Bonnie asked over dinner.

"Church?" he sputtered. Walt had dragged him to church a few times since arriving but it was by no means a regular outing for them. There was too much work on the ranch.

"Of course. It's our first Sunday here, and it's all arranged with your brothers. You didn't know?"

He'd holler at them later for springing it on him, but he could see how important it was for her to go. "It's no trouble, we just work most Sundays. It'll be a good chance to convince the others we're in love."

"Yes, of course," she said, averting her gaze. "So about the mercantile?"

"Naw, town shuts up tighter than a drum on Sundays. 'Cept the saloon, of course. That's always open."

Bonnie smirked. "Well, I don't suppose they stock furnishings and dry goods, do they?"

Bart laughed. "No dry goods there. Only wet. But I tell ya what. I'll take you ladies into town bright and early Monday morning. Then you can order the furniture and what-not you need to turn this shack into your home."

After the dinner dishes were done, Bonnie brought a small leather-covered book to the table, along with a pen and inkwell. When she opened the book, he saw it was blank, like a diary. She looked at him expectantly

"What's all this?"

"Bart, your stories are so wonderful, they should be written down. I thought I could write them as you tell them, since you don't seem keen on writing them yourself. What do you think?"

He still didn't think anyone outside his family would want to read them, but it sounded like a fun thing to do. Goodness knew he loved to tell his tales, and Bonnie seemed to love hearing them. What could it hurt?

"I think a chaparral fox is plumb foolish alongside you, Bonnie Blue."

Once again, he couldn't help feeling bad for his brothers that one of them didn't choose Bonnie. *Heck*, he thought, *just look at that smile!*

-11-

It was going to be a stressful day for Bonnie. Not only would she be meeting new people at church, but she'd have to pretend all day that she and Bart were happily married because all three couples were having a late lunch together at Nate's house.

It had been easy enough to fool her sisters into believing she and Bart were a real couple during their daily homemaking lessons, but this would be the first time spending any amount of time with them. If his brothers knew him half as well as her sisters knew her, they might suspect something. Of course, according to Bart, the triplets could practically read each others' minds, so she was worried they'd figure it out as soon as they saw them together.

With only two dresses to her name, there was only so much dressing up she could do. Once they went to town and bought some cloth, that would change, but for now, she would just have to deal with what she had. Tucking her hair up under her prettiest bonnet, she walked out of the bedroom.

She'd washed and mended all of Bart's clothes over the past week, and he looked smart in freshly pressed trousers and a blue wool shirt. He also looked confused.

"When did you find the time to do all the washing? Can't remember the last time this shirt was clean."

"So I noticed," she said, pinching her nose. "But you look quite handsome in that color, Bart."

He held his arm out for her. As she tucked hers into the crook, he said, "Hopefully that'll make it easier to pretend you're head over heels for me."

Bonnie was grateful he was looking away at the moment because she wasn't sure she'd be able to explain the blush creeping up her cheeks. What was wrong with her?

Bart, Nate and Walt all shouted to each other over the noise of their wagons on the hour-long ride into Wiggieville. Bonnie had never sat so close to a man before, but she wanted to put on a good show for her sisters. Whenever he made a joke, she smiled up at him.

For his part, Bart was very believable. Maybe a

little too believable. Whenever they walked together, if her arm wasn't looped through his, he kept one hand at the small of her back protectively. Every once in a while, she'd glance over to find him gazing at her. There was no other word for it but 'gazing'. No man had ever looked at her that way and, even though she knew it was fake, it made her stomach feel funny.

She caught both her sisters smiling in her direction more than once, so she was sure they believed the ruse. But would the brothers? They seemed too wrapped up in their own wives to pay much attention to her and Bart, which was just fine with Bonnie. The less they noticed the better.

The Wiggieville church was a small building filled with ranchers and farmers, along with a handful of women and children. The balance was definitely tipped in favor of men, and every man without a wife followed the Blue sisters' every move.

Well, not *all* the Blue sisters. The moment Bonnie stepped away from Gwen and Libby to meet a local furniture maker, she noticed that all those eyes stopped following her. Of course. They were watching her sisters. How could she have been so stupid?

Bart was so kind to her, and his acting skills were so good, that she almost thought for a moment she was attractive. Not that she wanted to draw the kind of attention Gwen often received, but for the first time in her life she'd felt...pretty.

How foolish!

"Joe Standish makes the best furniture in town, Bonnie." She barely heard Bart's words as he made introductions.

Why was she taking this so hard? The entire town of Beckham ignored her all her life; she should be used to it by now. Giving herself a mental slap, she tried to focus on Mr. Standish.

"How do you do, sir. I'm so glad to meet you because we're in desperate need of some furnishings." She smiled up at Bart, and gave his arm a squeeze. "My husband apparently didn't believe in furniture before I came along."

Bart wrapped an arm around her waist and hugged her to his side. "Yup, I was a barbarian before this little filly done tamed me."

Mr. Standish beamed at them. "By golly, miracles do happen! I never would have thought I'd see the day when Bart Dalton settled down. I figgered you'd be happily a-wanderin' around the desert like Moses for the rest of your life, son."

Bonnie didn't want to talk about Bart's drifter ways with strangers, so she glanced over to see how many more admirers her sisters had attracted. One man was standing much too close to Gwen, and Bonnie could see she was uncomfortable.

"Mr. Standish, would you please excuse me for a moment? I would like to discuss ordering some furniture from you but my sisters are also new in town and I want to see how they're faring."

Leaving Bart to talk with the furniture maker, Bonnie hurried up the aisle. Libby had noticed the man, too, and they both flanked Gwen just as she snatched her hand away from him.

"I'm a married woman, Mr. Jenkins," she said. Bonnie thought she sounded honestly upset by his attentions. This was a new side of her sister — normally Gwen would be lapping up his adoration like a kitten would milk.

"Men die young out here," he replied. "Just staking my claim." And with that horrible comment, he skulked off to the other side of the church, never letting Gwen out of his sight.

Understandably, Libby jumped all over Gwen for encouraging the scoundrel, but as far as Bonnie could tell, she'd done no such thing. Those two were always bickering and, as much as they might have grown over the last week, some things never changed.

"It was unfair to assume you'd done something wrong without knowing all the facts," she said, hinting to Libby to stop arguing with her sister in the house of God. Thankfully she took it.

The three couples settled on the same pew, offering Bonnie the chance to observe her sisters and their husbands more closely. Gwen looked quite happy, if a little unsure of herself, but Libby looked almost miserable.

Several times during the sermon, which just happened to be about marriage, Bonnie thought she saw tears in her sweet sister's eyes. Once, Libby caught her looking and quickly smiled to cover up whatever she was feeling. Nate was oblivious and looked nearly as troubled as his wife. Bonnie didn't like the look of that one little bit and made a mental note to have a private chat with Libby the next time they were alone.

"Proverbs 31:10 says, 'Who can find a virtuous woman?'" intoned the preacher. "'For her price is far above rubies.' God is telling us to seek out a good woman, a noble wife, because she will bring more to your life than a sackful of riches."

Several men in the congregation shouted, "Hear hear!" None of them had women by their sides.

"'The heart of her husband doth safely trust in her, so that he shall have no need of spoil.' When you have such a woman by your side, helping you, supporting you, you can trust her. By trusting her fully, your life will be enriched beyond measure."

"Amen, preacher!"

"'She will do him good and not evil all the days of her life.' How many of you today have found such a treasure? Say amen!"

A handful of men responded, including Bart. His loud 'Amen!' made her jump and she couldn't stop herself from smiling at him. He returned the smile and winked.

Right, it was part of the act. Of course.

-12-

The couples had lunch at Nate's. His place was the most comfortable and, for the first time, Bart appreciated his brother's efforts to make a home out of the cozy shack they'd built together. Of course, Bonnie cooked, and he sent a silent prayer of thanks for that. He'd heard plenty from his brothers about their wives' kitchen skills — or lack of them.

As soon as they were all seated around the table, Walt piped up to pray. Naturally. As their self-appointed leader, he would jump in and pray for all of them, even though they were in Nate's home and Bart's wife had done the cooking.

Any irritation he felt evaporated when he realized he'd just thought of Bonnie as his wife. She was his house manager, not his wife. Not really. Why was his mind playing tricks on him like that?

She was the one who'd suggested the arrangement in the first place, after all. And it would be downright cruel to pursue any amorous feelings he might have for her because he would be leaving sooner or later. She didn't deserve that, even if she did want a more traditional marriage, which he doubted.

Stop thinking that way! he chided himself. Libby was asking about him and he could barely focus. He was pretty sure she wanted to know about his past.

"I left home at seventeen," he said, giving his brothers a knowing look. His departure had hurt them, but they supported his decision anyway. He would always love them for that. "I don't know why, but I just couldn't stay there any longer. My feet have always been itchy."

Walt's wife — the really beautiful, kind of dumb one — asked, "Why do your feet itch?"

Really? Walt must be kicking himself daily for choosing as he did. He would have been so much happier with Bonnie. The very idea twisted up Bart's guts and he pushed it out of his mind. He didn't like the thought of that one little bit.

He sighed, as much in response to his own emotions as Gwen's question. "It's an expression. I have a hard time staying in one place for a long time. I prefer to move around and see new things. I hate seeing the same thing day in and day out."

Gwen's eyes grew round as she looked between

him and Bonnie, as if Bonnie didn't already know. She used the word 'rambler' to describe him, which was irksome. He was a drifter, not a rambler. To his way of thinking, there was a mighty big difference between the two, though he'd be hard-pressed to explain it to someone.

Thankfully Gwen moved on to prying into Nate's past, but Bart was left wondering if he'd done the right thing by talking about himself like that. Would Bonnie's sisters give her grief over it?

Sure, they were pretending their marriage was real, but he didn't want to lie about who he was. He'd be leaving one of these days anyway, so might as well get everyone used to the notion.

Bart risked a quick glance at Bonnie to gauge her reaction to the conversation. She was smiling, but there was something about it that didn't set quite right with him, like it didn't reach her eyes. Then he got a good look at her eyes and swore he saw a tear welling in one just as she turned her head.

He almost convinced himself they were happy tears. Almost.

Once again, Bart didn't waste the chance to remind Bonnie of where she stood in his life. Did he really have to blab so freely about his wandering ways? She'd hoped to keep the charade going for a little while. People had pitied her all of her life, and now she had the chance to at least pretend she was happy.

To be honest, she was happy, for the most part. Her sisters were quickly learning how to be good homemakers, and they'd even offered to help spruce up her little shack of a cabin with curtains, if she taught them how to sew. Spring gardens were already planned out, and they would yield enough food to feed them all for months. And she'd spent hours setting up a bookkeeping system for Bart's part of the ranch. Apparently the man thought an old cigar box with chicken-scratch notes was enough to run a budding empire!

Even she and Bart got along quite well. Every night was spent writing out his adventures, which were simply thrilling. He had a wonderful wit and she felt quite at ease with him. Considering the rough start they'd had, she was thrilled they'd become friends.

Later that night, as she lay in her bed alone, listening to Bart's snores from the other room, she wondered what it would be like when he went on one of his safaris. Worry gripped her. She'd never been left alone to protect herself before and, for the first time, realized she needed to know how to handle a gun. She added 'Learn to shoot' to the top of her list for the next day.

"Of course, I'll teach you to shoot," Bart said the next morning over breakfast. He was more impressed with Bonnie every day. Nate had told him Libby was terrified to learn to ride a horse, and here was her older sister asking to be taught to shoot. The woman had a good head on her shoulders. "You need to learn to ride, too?"

"Sort of. I learned to ride side saddle some but that doesn't seem practical out here. Besides, I would bet good money you don't even own a side saddle."

"Good guess, Bonnie Blue. Out here, common sense is more important than good manners. It'd be mighty hard to outrun a pack of wolves riding side saddle."

She nodded, a determined look on her face.

"We'll try some target practice today when we get back from town, sound good? We could also order up a side saddle, if'n that's what you really want."

Bonnie's smile warmed him, but her words stunned him. "No, I trust your judgment." No one had ever said that to him in his life, and it made him feel strange inside, like she was depending on him. He wasn't sure how he felt about that.

A familiar itch started in his big toe.

-13-

As they started the ride into Wiggieville, Bonnie pretended she was in love with Bart by clutching his arm. The ropey muscles under his duster flexed and jumped as he twitched the reins, and she had to admit she liked how they felt. It was strange how comfortable she was touching this man.

Her sisters were seated in the back on a board Bart had set up so they wouldn't have to sprawl in the wagon bed. Not like she had to do on the day of her wedding. Gwen and Libby talked almost nonstop about all the goods they were going to buy in town and she could feel Bart silently laughing.

"I'm going to find the prettiest dress, maybe even a cornflower blue one," Gwen declared.

"I want a new dress, too," Libby whined.

"Ooh, maybe we can find a confectioner who carries Swiss chocolates," cooed Gwen. Libby responded with her own coo.

As her sisters bickered and blabbered in the back, Bart handed Bonnie the reins without a word. Her heart started beating faster but she took them without question, praying she didn't get them all killed. After a few jerks and swerves, though, she got the hang of it, and drove until they reached the outskirts of Wiggieville. It was a relief when Bart took the reins back, as there were a lot of things to dodge in town, but she was proud of herself for handling the rig so well. Her sisters hadn't suspected a thing.

"I'll wait in the wagon," Bart said as he helped her sisters down.

They scurried ahead of her toward Wiggieville's small mercantile while she waited for Bart to help her, too. The excitement of driving a team of horses — even just two — must have been too much for her because when she tried to step down off the buckboard, she lost her footing and fell right into his arms.

He caught her deftly and held her body against his for just a moment longer than was strictly necessary before letting her slide slowly to the ground. He was staring into her eyes and she was helpless to look away.

"You alright, Bonnie Blue?" he breathed, one hand burning a brand on her waist, the other brushing a loose curl of hair from her cheek.

Why couldn't she speak? Why couldn't she breath? Why couldn't she *move*?

Bart's gaze drifted down to her lips and his head moved forward almost imperceptibly. Bonnie sucked in a gulp of air. He was going to kiss her!

"Bonnie, are you coming?" Gwen's irritated voice echoed down the street. "You can kiss your new husband later!"

Bart blinked, Bonnie gasped and the moment passed. Adjusting his hat, he gave her a curt nod and strode down the street without a word. Only when the dizziness passed did she dare take a step toward the store.

What had he been thinking?! The trouble was, he hadn't been. He'd simply reacted to her, and that could only lead to hurt feelings and trouble down the road. He didn't want to screw this up, not just for his own sake but for Bonnie's, too. Toying with her affections would only get her all mixed up, and the last thing he wanted to do was hurt her.

He needed a walk. They'd be in the mercantile for some time, he reckoned, though he was certain his sisters-in-law were going to be sorely disappointed at the selection. He'd be mighty surprised if ol' Mr. Fisher stocked Swiss chocolates in there. They'd be lucky to find sugar on some days.

Bart couldn't help smiling as he ambled through the little town. He'd drifted though dozens, probably hundreds of tiny towns and big cities, from Oregon City to New York City, but there was something special about Wiggieville.

The false-front buildings lining Main Street were all the rage, and he thought he'd never grow tired of the architectural style. Flower boxes decorated the buildings in the more upstanding part of town, which always brightened his spirits. And everyone just seemed happy there.

As he passed the Burnt Pickle Saloon, he considered stopping in for a quick drink but he didn't want Bonnie smelling whiskey on his breath. Since moving to his new homestead, he'd made a number of trips to town for supplies and socializing. He didn't spend a lot of time at the saloon, but he wasn't a total stranger either.

The doors swung open and out stumbled the town rummy, an old scoundrel by the name of Winston. The poor fella was too old to get a regular job anymore, so he did odd jobs around town and the surrounding ranches, and spent his earnings at the saloon.

"Burt, my ol' pal!" His words were slurred but understandable. Must be a few days till payday.

"Winston, how are you, ya ol' hound dog?"

"S'alright," mumbled, swaying where he stood. "Hey, I hear ya done gone off and got hitched."

Bart smiled and shrugged noncommittally. Forget the old busybodies in the sewing circle, Winston was the biggest gossip in town. You didn't say a word to him that you didn't want everyone in town to hear.

"Whatchya go and do that fer? Ya git some chickadee in trouble?"

Bart bristled at the old man's suggestion that Bonnie might be anything other than virtuous, even though he knew Winston had never met her. It was nothing personal, he reminded himself.

"No, sir, not at all. In fact, she's a fine woman."

"Huh. Guess she'd halfta be to git a drifter like you to settle down. Too bad. Always dreamed o' taggin' along witchya on one o' yer...whatchamacallits?"

"Safaris," Bart muttered, not at all cottoning to the thought of going on safari with Winston. The old lush had drifted around himself over the years, and certainly knew the ropes, but Bart liked to be alone on his little adventures. That was the whole point.

"Yeah, that's them! Bah, it wouldn't work out no how. You and me? We're loners, Burt."

"Bart," he corrected, but Winston ignored him. His slurring was getting worse.

"We're the same, you'n me. I feel bad fer that new wife o' yers, cuz one o' these days, she's gonna end up jest like my three wives. Alone and wondering where the Sam Hill you got off to."

At that, he cackled with glee. Bart couldn't believe

what he was hearing. Winston had never mentioned being married before, much less three times.

"You had three wives?" Bart was astounded.

"Have," Winston corrected. "They're still out there somewheres, I reckon."

"What happened? Why'd you leave?"

"You know why, boy. We got the same itchy feet, you 'n me."

Winston squinted at him hard. For a brief moment, he stopped swaying and focused entirely on Bart. It sent a shiver down Bart's spine.

"Watch yerself, Burt, or one day, not too long from now, you'll end up jest like me."

With that, he resumed swaying and stumbled away, apparently forgetting he'd been in the middle of a conversation. Winston disappeared down a side street, leaving Bart swaying in his place.

-14-

Bart hardly said a word on the ride back to the shared ranch. Bonnie wondered if he was angry at how much she'd bought and ordered in town, but he'd said she could get whatever she needed. She certainly hadn't bought anything frivolous, but the final bill was a fair bit more than what either of her sister's purchased. Of course, they had fully furnished homes so that shouldn't have been surprising.

No, something else was bothering him, she could tell, and the only thing that made sense was the almost-kiss. He must have regretted even thinking about kissing the likes of her, and now he was pulling away to not lead her on. Either that, or she misread the whole situation entirely and had only imagined he was about to kiss her.

Whatever was going on, he sat on the far side of the seat from her and didn't once let her take the reins. Her sisters went on and on about the bolts of fabric and supplies they bought, and how Bonnie was going to teach them to sew, and Thanksgiving dinner, and on and on.

"Bonnie, that wardrobe you ordered is just lovely," Libby said at some point.

Bart shot her a look. "You bought furniture?"

She gnawed on her lip, worried that she'd made him mad. They'd been getting along so well and now...

"Only the wardrobe. I...I need someplace to put my clothes. Is that a problem?"

"Naw, I just didn't realize you were ordering furniture. Is that it?"

Her hackles raised at his strange mood. "For now," she said defiantly.

She caught his small smirk out of the corner of her eye. Maybe he wasn't mad after all. And why did she care anyway? She was managing his homestead, and the place needed to be furnished. Either he trusted her or he didn't. She crossed her arms in a huff and refused to look at him until they got home.

Bart waited till he'd dropped off Bonnie's sisters before he spoke again. Clearly his chat with Winston had rattled him, but he wasn't sure why. The old bugger was always going off like that. Then when he asked Bonnie a simple question, she got mad at him. Having been on the receiving end of her sharp tongue before, he decided to play it safe and shut his trap for the rest of the ride.

But as soon as they pulled up in front of their cabin, he asked, "Ready for your shooting lesson?"

He caught her off guard and he liked the way she blinked at him in confusion. "Excuse me?"

"Your shooting lesson, remember? We can put all this away later. If you promise not to blow my head off, I'll teach you how to shoot a shotgun."

She tried not to laugh, he could tell, but she couldn't stop from giggling. Just hearing her laugh made him feel better. Whatever had gotten into him was gone. He didn't like feeling all mixed up.

Out back of the barn, Bart set a hay bale on end and paced back fifty steps. Bonnie paid close attention when he loaded and unloaded the shotgun, and imitated him perfectly on her first try. She had a little trouble pulling back the hammer, but quickly figured out a way to do it more efficiently without having to rely on brute strength. Hoo boy, she was a smart one.

"Okay, now see those two notches? You sight down the barrel till they line up, then you just pull the trigger."

BLAM!

Not a single speck of hay went flying. She'd missed

completely. His ears were still ringing when he realized Bonnie was flat on her back. The gun had knocked the tiny little thing over completely!

"You hurt, Bonnie Blue?" A flash of anxiety ran through him but eased when he saw the determined glint in her eye. He didn't even have time to give her a hand up before she was back on her feet, aiming the gun.

"Now hold on one second. That there was the shotgun's kick. Almost as bad as a mule's. Ya gotta brace that shoulder hard and maybe plant your feet a little wider. Then lean into it when you're ready to shoot. Atta girl! Now try again."

BLAM!

She still missed the hay bale completely, but at least this time she stayed on her feet. The fierce grin on her face and the wild look in her eyes gave him a moment's pause before he handed over more shells.

"Be careful, that barrel's hot," he warned. It took a minute for her to reload but she did it all on her own.

"Ready?" she asked. He stifled a chuckle and nodded.

BLAM!

A small corner of the bale disappeared in a puff of hay. "Again." He didn't have to say it twice.

BLAM!

This time the entire bale tumbled over, a fine dusting of hay fluttering all around it. "You did it!" he cried, sweeping her up in his arms.

She laughed and did her best not to drop the gun as he spun her around. Setting her on her feet, he looked down at her. Her eyes were sparkling like the gems they resembled and her cheeks were a fetching shade of pink.

His finger moved of its own accord to stroke one, but he stopped himself. No sense going down that road again. Instead, he wrapped an arm around her shoulder and gave her a friendly side-hug.

"You're a natural, Bonnie Blue. I won't have to worry about you a bit when I'm out on safari. Now you get to learn how to clean the thing."

-15-

Aside from the strange tension on the ride home, Bonnie had the best day of her life. She scratched off several items from her to-do list during that one trip to Wiggieville, she drove a wagon team *and* she learned to shoot a gun. Bart even showed her how to hitch and unhitch the wagon a few times.

"Easy," she declared, to which Bart smiled.

"That's my Bonnie Blue!"

A glow warmed her tummy at his praise. He even complimented her on her good sense when they unpacked all the supplies she bought. She showed him in the record book she started how much each item cost and the running tally of his finances. She didn't really consider it 'their' finances because her job was to simply manage it.

Once things settled down and her sisters didn't need so much help, she'd probably start a sewing business or some such thing to earn her own spending money. Trinkets and frilly things never appealed to her much, but Mr. Fisher had a beautiful tortoise shell hair set that caught her eye.

"You should buy it," Gwen had urged. "You deserve it."

A remnant of bitterness welled in her at the comment because her mother had gifted an heirloom set very much like it to Gwen, when by all rights she should have given it to the oldest daughter.

"She needs it more than you," was all Mama said when Bonnie brought up the subject. It was all she needed to say because her meaning was clear: Bonnie was too homely for anything to make her look attractive.

She'd never spend so much of Bart's money on such a thing, as it wasn't necessary to the running of the house, but she couldn't deny wanting to own it. Besides, who would she try to attract? For all intents and purposes, Bart was her employer. But since she also happened to be married to him, it wasn't like she could flirt with other men.

Shaking the bad thoughts from her head, she focused on all the food she now had to choose from. A nice roast with her special roasted root vegetables and a pie for dessert sounded like a wonderful way to celebrate such a wonderful day.

Under Bonnie's direction, Bart put away all the goods she bought in town. There'd never been so much food in his little cabin before and he boggled at it all. They could survive the winter on those stores alone, but she insisted they'd have to make another trip to town in a few weeks to replenish. He shook his head in wonder and bit his tongue.

It wasn't the money. Lord knew he had plenty since the ranch had already turned a small profit and he had nothing to spend it on. Bart had wanted his brothers to keep most of it, or at least put it back into the ranch, but Walt had insisted he put it away for "a rainy day," he'd said.

It suddenly dawned on him that Walt had planned on ordering up wives for them from the very beginning! That's why he wanted Bart to save his money. That's why he was always nagging him to make or buy some furniture. He wanted to trap Bart into staying put. *Why, that dagblamed, no-good sonofa—*

"Supper's ready," Bonnie chimed, interrupting his internal rant.

He was still fuming at his belated realization that he'd been played for a chump from the moment he answered Walt's letter, but he did his best to put on a happy face. The roast she laid on the little table smelled delicious, and she served her famous fluffy mashed potatoes. Again.

"Mashed taters again, huh?"

She gaped at him for a second while he plopped a spoonful onto his plate and stabbed a slice of the meat. "I-I-I thought you liked my potatoes."

He shrugged and stuffed some into his mouth, instantly regretting taking his frustration with Walt out on her. Her cooking was the best he'd ever had, and he looked forward to it.

"Sorry, I'm just cross with Walt. I could eat your taters every day for the rest of my life."

Her frown eased and her cheeks flushed. Dropping her gaze, she spun around and hurried back to the kitchen. He wondered what that was about. If he didn't know better, he'd think she was love-struck or something.

As he chewed in silence, his thoughts bounced from Walt to Winston to Bonnie and back again. He couldn't make head nor tails from any of it sitting here in the cabin. The soles of his feet itched something fierce.

Pushing back from the table, he said, "I need to go check on Roamer. Mighty fine meal, Bonnie Blue. Sorry again for gettin' testy with you."

Before she could say a word, he was out the door and headed for the barn.

The moment he stepped in the barn, he felt he could breathe again. Roamer whinnied at him, no doubt scolding him for leaving him behind every day. Bart grabbed the curry comb and started stroking his old friend.

"Sorry, Roamer, but I was just looking out for that hoof o' yours. 'Sides, Dimple Junior needed some time in the fields."

The old chestnut chuffed at him in response. "Yeah, you wanna get outta this ol' pen, dontchya? You want to feel the dirt under your feet again, amiright?"

As he brushed, he thought about what he'd said to Bonnie, and it hit him. He'd said he could eat her food every night for the rest of his life.

The rest of his life.

Panic seized him and stilled his hand. It was a figure of speech! He hadn't meant it! She had to know he wasn't going to be around forever. That was their understanding, and the whole thing had been her idea from the beginning!

He couldn't deny he was attracted to Bonnie, and he'd almost kissed her in town, but he wasn't the marrying kind. A man like him would never settle down. He was too busy being a drifter. Or he had been, before Walt tricked him.

The sound of boots scuffing dirt outside the barn drew his attention away from his panicked thoughts. He peered over the stall door, praying Walt would walk in so he could jump the conniving bully like a roadrunner on a rattler. But it was Nate's head that popped around the corner.

"Evenin', brother," Nate said as he ambled in. "Heard some shootin' over here earlier. Thought maybe that smart wife of yours finally wised up and shot ya, but here you are."

Bart grimaced. "Naw, I was just teachin' her to shoot. She needs to know how to protect herself when I'm gone on safari."

Nate blinked at him. "Safari? You ain't fixin' to leave again, are ya? It's only been a week, Bart. I thought things were going good 'twixt you two. You always seem thicker than thieves."

Bart resisted the urge to scratch his ankle. His brothers knew the signs when he was ready to hightail it out of there, and he didn't want a lecture. "Things are jest fine, Nate. I'm just sayin'...a woman needs to know how to handle a gun out here, is all."

Nate scratched his head and looked a little irritated. "How'd she take to it?"

Bart had to chuckle. Bonnie Blue was a natural. "Like a duck to water, brother. That's the way she is with pert-near everything."

"Well, next time give us a little warning, would ya? I was trying to teach Libby to ride and the gunshots spooked poor ol' Jack. Nearly sent my poor wife flying, but she managed to hang on. Not sure if'n I'll get her near a horse again anytime soon, though."

"Sorry, Nate. I shoulda thought o' that."

His brother shrugged, dug his toe in the dirt and fell silent for a few minutes. That wasn't strange between them. Being quiet with his brothers was the most comfortable thing in the world to Bart. To all of them.

"Well, I best get back," Nate finally said, but he gave Bart a stern look before leaving. "I got two things to say to you first, brother. One, you're a grown man now and ain't nobody can make you do nothin' you don't want, deep down. Two, you got yerself a fine woman there. Don't be stupid."

Bart could only gape after him.

-16-

Bonnie woke up in a fine mood the next morning. Tomorrow she planned to teach her sisters to sew, and they'd kindly offered to make curtains for her home their first project. She'd been so touched by the gesture because it was probably the first time they both made an effort to help her, instead of the other way around.

She'd always loved her sisters, but all too often it was because she had to. They were her sisters, after all. But this trip had somehow brought them closer than ever, and in her morning prayer, she gave extra thanks for that.

As she performed her morning ablutions, she thought on Bart's words the night before. "I could eat your taters every day for the rest of my life," he'd said.

Was he trying to tell her he wasn't going to leave in

a year's time after all? That he wanted to make things between them more permanent? She was almost certain he'd been about to kiss her in town, plus he seemed to genuinely like her. Then again, maybe he was just being nice and complimenting her on her potatoes.

She'd come up with a clever way to bring it up again but he didn't come back from the barn before it was time for her to go to bed. No matter, they could always talk about it over breakfast.

Licking a finger, she smoothed a stray hair back into place and regarded her appearance in the small hand mirror she bought in town. Her color was higher than normal, which gave her pretty pink cheeks. After lightly chewing on her lips, they looked full and rosy. Every button was done and her skirts were smooth. This was as good as it got, so she might as well see if Bart was up.

As usual, the cabin was dark when she stepped out of her room. Bart never woke up until she had coffee and breakfast on the stove. She didn't even bother trying to be quiet anymore because the man could sleep through a tornado.

She lit the new lamp she bought on her shopping trip. It was going to be a treat to have two lamps to light the kitchen this morning. Bart had kindly filled all three lamps she brought home, plus the one in her bedroom, the night before. That increasingly familiar warmth filled her chest, and she glanced over to his sleeping form and smiled.

Her smile faltered. *What...?* The cabin was small, but the oil lamps only threw so much light, and in the flickering darkness, she wasn't sure what she was looking at. It was off to the side of where Bart usually slept, and didn't look much like a sleeping man.

Stepping closer, she could see that Bart wasn't there at all. His bedroll was gone, too. The bulk she saw in the shadows was a big pile of chopped wood, with a piece of paper on top fluttering around under a piece of kindling.

Cold sunk in to her belly as she reached for it. Her shaking hand made it impossible to read so she moved over to the table. She had a sudden urge to sit down anyway.

Spreading the note flat on the table and setting the lamp next to it, she started to read.

Bonnie Blue,

By the time you read this, me and Roamer will be off on another safari. We should only be gone a few days, a week at the outside, and I feel strongly that you can handle anything that comes along. That shotgun will keep the worst of what's out here at bay, and now you have a fully stocked larder so you ain't going hungry. Hope you don't mind but I took the leftover meat and bread. Wish I could have took your

*taters, too, but they'd make a mess of my saddlebag.
I cut up this wood for you so you wouldn't have to. If
you run out, just ask Nate or Walt to cut some more.
My brothers are used to my safaris but you can tell
your sisters I'm off on business, if you want.*

   Kind Regards,
   Bart Dalton

The final words grew blurry and it wasn't until a
drop splattered on 'Kind Regards' that Bonnie realized
she had tears in her eyes. Fiercely wiping them away,
she chided herself for being silly.

"No need to be scared, Bonnie," she mumbled as
she went back to the kitchen. "You'll be just fine. You
know how to shoot and hitch the wagon and feed
yourself. There's nothing at all to be afraid of."

Then why was she trembling?

Bart breathed deeply as the sun crested over the
prairie. This is where he belonged. Not cooped up in
some little shack, working a ranch. He was a drifter,
proud and free. Nothing would ever change that.

He kept Roamer's pace slow and easy, not wanting
to further aggravate his hoof. Over the last week or so
— had it only been that long? — Bart had only let the
handsome chestnut walk around the corral for a little
exercise. After a day or two, he was no longer favoring

that leg and started snorting to be allowed to get busy.

But Bart insisted on using Dimple Junior for work, wanting to give Roamer more time to heal up. The split would have to grow out, of course, and the less he was worked, the less likely it would be to split more. Now the old fella was itching to have free rein and run, but Bart kept him moving slow.

He still couldn't believe it had been a little over a week since Walt had suckered him into marrying a mail-order bride! Just thinking on it raised his hackles. Why did his 'big brother' think he knew what was best for everyone? When was he going to get it through his thick skull that they were all grown men and could make their own decisions?

He spent the day fuming on the injustice of it all as they made their way to his favorite little camping spot. It was tucked under some trees next to a sweet little creek and was a great place for thinking.

Normally, he wouldn't get set up till close to nightfall, but he'd left so early, he was hunkered over the campfire by mid-afternoon. Roamer had drunk deeply from the creek and seemed happy enough to be done for the day. Bart felt the same.

It was good to be back out here. There was nothing quite like lying under the stars alone at night to make a man understand his place in this world. He was a speck of nothing, and if he disappeared, pert-much no one would notice the difference. No one relied on him and that was fine by him.

Hunger started gnawing at his belly so he unpacked the food he brought. As soon as he smelled the meat frying in his little pan, his thoughts turned to Bonnie. A part of him regretted leaving her like that, without so much as a goodbye, but she'd proven she could take care of herself. She didn't need him.

Besides, she might as well get used to him coming and going because, soon enough, he'd be gone for good. He'd made a promise to his brothers, and he intended on keeping it, but then he and Roamer would hightail it out of there. Bonnie could take care of his portion of the homestead and keep all the profits, as far as he was concerned. She'd deserve them.

By the time dark fell, his belly was full and he had a nice pile of firewood. Roamer was fed and resting quietly nearby. In the firelight, Bart thought he saw the horse favoring that leg again. He'd check it in the morning.

Lying back on his bedroll, he tucked his hands under his head and watched the flickering glow of the leaves swaying above him, stars popping through with the movement. Many more leaves had fallen since his last visit. With a start, he realized that had been his wedding day.

He snorted. Some wedding. Walt had blindsided him, making him feel responsible for the poor gal standing all alone on that platform. His brother hadn't left him any choice but to marry her.

And what choice did Bonnie have? They'd had enough conversations for him to know that she would have been in a hard spot if he hadn't agreed to her plan. What would have become of her if he'd just walked away?

She probably would have made her way home, but then she would have been forced to marry that filthy old man. She deserved so much better than that. In fact, she deserved better than what she had, but she seemed to prefer it over the other option.

As Bart drifted off to sleep, the rustling leaves overhead and all around him formed whispers in his mind. A lady's whispers. Whispers he couldn't quite make out. He strained to hear the words. A few times, he almost caught what she was saying but then the words flitted away. Slumber settled over him like a warm blanket, sweet whispers echoing in his ears.

-17-

Bonnie got control of herself long before she went over to Gwen's. Both sisters' skills were improving greatly every day, and this day Gwen made her very first batch of bread on her own. Of course, Bonnie watched but her once-lazy, spoiled sister managed two perfect loaves without a word of instruction.

She and Libby couldn't help giggling as Gwen danced around the cabin in celebration. Then she stopped and gave Bonnie a kiss on the cheek, exclaiming, "You're a wonderful teacher, Bonnie!"

Bonnie felt a swell of pride, not only for her ability to teach but at Gwen and Libby's growth. Gwen always seemed overly confident, but she was secretly so afraid of failing that she'd barely been trying to learn how to cook. Poor little Libby, on the other hand, wanted to learn but was so insecure she kept second-guessing herself.

Regardless of their inner conflicts, both of her sisters were becoming wonderful homemakers. There was no doubt in her mind that they would have long and happy marriages with their husbands, as soon as Libby fully adjusted. The pained smile she plastered on her face when Gwen went on and on about how happy she was was a dead giveaway. But unless Libby broached the subject, Bonnie wasn't about to stick her nose in.

"What are we cooking for dinner tonight?" Gwen demanded.

Now was as good a time as any to tell her sisters Bart was gone. She shrugged as casually as she could and said, "Bart's away for a few days on a business trip, so I'll probably just have a sandwich."

Only after she said it did she remember that Bart took all the cooked meat and bread with him. Darn him!

Of course this revelation brought a round of questioning from her concerned — and clearly relieved — sisters. They didn't want their husbands leaving them in the wilds of Texas alone, and Bonnie couldn't blame them. For them, it could be a death sentence. Luckily, Bonnie was more self-reliant.

Thankfully the subject quickly turned back to dinner, and Bonnie showed her sisters how to make a delicious potato soup. They were fast learners and insisted on doing as much as they could to help. She was quite grateful because, for some reason, she was tired to her bones. If she laid her head down, she was certain she'd be out till the next morning.

As she and Libby were getting ready to leave, Gwen asked her to stay for supper. "No, thank you," was on her lips when she remembered she had no leftovers. It didn't make sense to make a big meal for just one person, plus it was getting late.

"Walt won't mind?"

"Of course not," Gwen insisted, though Bonnie thought she saw a flicker of doubt in her eye. "Please come."

"I'd be happy to. I have something for you anyway. Let me run home and get it."

During her meager free time, Bonnie had been working on Gwen's cornflower blue dress. She'd nearly thrown a hissy fit when she discovered her favorite dress hadn't been packed in their rush to escape Beckham, and the bolt of blue cloth had been the first thing Gwen bought at the mercantile. It wasn't as fancy as her previous dress, but she would appreciate the practicality of this one very soon. At least she'd better.

Bonnie was pleasantly surprised at her reaction. "Oh Bonnie! It's perfect. When did you find the time? We're working morning to night."

That was true, but Bonnie could do her chores much more quickly, plus she didn't have a husband who was carrying her off to the bedroom every evening. "I can always find a little time," was all she'd say.

While Gwen was trying it on, Walt came in, looking tired and irritable. "You didn't have to cook for us, Bonnie."

"I didn't! Gwen cooked, I just supervised. She invited me to stay for supper because Bart is on his business trip."

She gave him a knowing look and emphasized the last two words so he would understand not to spill the beans to Gwen. He raised an eyebrow at her but was quickly distracted when Gwen came out in her new dress. She looked beautiful.

Bonnie looked down at her mud-brown work dress and sighed. Gwen's hair tumbled prettily around her face, while her own was tucked up tight in a bun. Gwen's lips and cheeks were naturally pink, while she had to pinch and bite her own to achieve such a glow. No wonder she'd been picked last. No wonder Bart left.

A single tear plopped in the soup.

"I'll walk you home," Walt said after dinner.

All she wanted was to be alone and was about to object, but she didn't want to insult her new brother-in-law. "I'd appreciate that."

As they walked the short distance to Bart's — *her* — cabin, Walt cleared his throat. "Erm, you know Bart ain't on no business trip, right?"

The pity in his voice irked her. "Of course, I know, Walt. There are no secrets between Bart and me."

She'd tried to sound confident, but it came across sounding snide. He just shrugged.

"I'm sorry for being terse," she finally said as they were approaching her cabin. "But I think it would be easiest for everyone if you could go along with the story."

He gave her a hard look. "I won't lie to my wife, Bonnie."

"No no! I wouldn't think of asking you to do that, but I'm sure Gwen won't bring it up on her own..."

Finally, he nodded. "If she don't ask, I won't tell. Fair enough?"

"Thank you," she breathed with relief.

"But..." he started, then stopped himself.

"Go on," she urged, not truly wanting him to continue.

"*Is* it fair? To you?

She pursed her lips and tipped her chin up. "I'm quite satisfied with my situation. Thank you for your concern."

Spinning on her heel, she walked through her door and closed it firmly. How dare the overbearing brute stick his nose in her business! Once he soundly rejected her at the train station, he gave up all rights to interfere in her life. She was absolutely fine.

So why was she trembling again?

-18-

Bart woke up with the sun after a night of disturbing dreams. He'd been trying to find something — a hat, he thought — but every time he got close, it disappeared. He'd never really thought much about hats before, but he really wanted this one. He was desperate to have it, but he could only catch glimpses of it. At one point, it was sitting right in front of him but when he reached for it, it turned into a blue mockingbird and flew away.

Why on earth was he dreaming about hats turning into birds? Normally when he was out on safari, he had peaceful dreams he rarely remembered, if he dreamt at all. He couldn't figure it out and it put him in a sour mood all morning.

Eating didn't hold any appeal so he just stoked the fire and brewed some strong coffee in the same pan he'd cooked dinner the night before. While it was brewing, he checked on Roamer, who was favoring his bad foot a little, just as he suspected.

"Hang it all," Bart muttered, angry at himself for pushing ol' Roamer when he knew the horse wasn't as young as he used to be. He rubbed some McLean's Volcanic Oil liniment from Roamer's hock to fetlock and hoped a day of rest would help. He'd planned to get some more miles under him, but he didn't want to risk the horse coming up lame.

Settling himself on a log in front of the fire, he took a sip of his coffee. "Gack!" He nearly spit it out but managed to swallow it. Out on the trail, drifters would call coffee this bad coffin varnish. Bart figured real coffin varnish would taste a might better than this brew.

Why was it so bad? It was the same coffee he used last time, same pan, same water. Yet it tasted bitter and foul. He threw it out and made a fresh batch. Maybe he let it boil too long. That could ruin a good cuppa mud.

After the long night of fitful sleep, he needed the coffee so he was careful to not let it sit on the fire too long. He slowly poured the brew into his mug, making sure to keep most of the grounds out. Raising the mug to his lips, he breathed deeply.

"Ahhhh," he sighed. There was nothing so fine as enjoying a good cup of coffee in front of the campfire.

There was something magical about it. The steaming black liquid was hot on his tongue but he ignored the little bite of pain. He was desperate!

"Bleck!" he cried, spitting it out this time. It was worse than the first batch. What the...?

He stared into the black depths, wondering why his coffee tasted so bad all of a sudden. Then it dawned on him. He'd been drinking Bonnie's delicious coffee long enough that he was spoiled. This swill couldn't compare to hers.

"Well, you better get used to it, fool," he muttered, bracing himself for another sip of the vile brew. It took a good half-hour but he managed to finally choke it all down, in spite of himself.

He was a drifter, through and through, and drifters lived hard lives, dagnabit. They slept on the ground, drank bitter coffee and were lucky to find decent meals. After just a few days, he was as mollycoddled as a newborn! This wouldn't do. Nope, not one little bit.

Digging a piece of jerky from his saddlebag, he sat by the creek and gnawed on it. Might as well have been chewing on rawhide, but he was determined not to eat the rest of Bonnie's leftovers. He had something to prove to himself.

He guessed he was grateful that he'd been sleeping on the floor since she arrived. It was harder than the ground, at least out here where the leaves had fallen and formed a nice bit of padding. The campfire kept him just as warm as the fireplace, too. Yup, being in the great outdoors was where he belonged.

Since he wouldn't be going anywhere that day, he decided to try a little hunting. A rabbit would make a nice supper. Besides, his legs needed stretching after riding most of the day before.

All day, he wandered around, trying to figure out all the nonsense spinning around in his head. It was a jumbled mess that he couldn't make heads nor tails of, and that made him sore. What it boiled down to, he figured, was that he hated everyone.

He was still angry with Walt for being his overbearing, know-it-all self and forcing him into a marriage he didn't want. Nate made the list by sticking his nose in his business the night before. Bonnie didn't do anything wrong that he could think of, but he was mad at her, too. And her silly sisters who were so spoiled that she had to teach them like children. Why couldn't they be more like her? How was it possible they were raised by the same parents?

Bonnie was whip-smart, knew how to cook better than anyone he'd ever known and had a unique beauty her sisters couldn't hold a candle to. Why his brothers fawned and drooled all over those other two was beyond Bart. Bonnie was the real prize, they were just chuckleheads who couldn't see it.

He had to admit, Gwen and Libby weren't all bad. Gwen was full of life and, after a few days, she seemed to really want to be a good wife. And Walt seemed to think she was sweet as Bonnie's apple pie. Nate had always been a closed book, but Bart could tell he was already devoted to his new bride, even though Libby seemed scared and unsure of everything. If he was being honest, he had to admit he rather liked his sisters-in-law.

Bart took a couple pot shots at a battered old cactus, imagining Nate's face. He'd spent his entire life being bossed around by his 'older' brother because everyone seemed to expect it. He'd heard Pa tell Walt once that it was his duty to watch out for his brothers because he was oldest. Didn't matter that they were triplets and born just minutes apart.

It was easy when they were kids. Bart didn't have to make too many decisions for himself, and if he got in trouble, Walt took the brunt of the punishment because he was oldest and "should know better." Eventually, though, that chafed Bart. He'd never be responsible for himself if he was around Walt, so he took off.

He'd spent a decade with no one to answer to but to himself, and that was fine by him. Making his own decisions suited him. If he screwed up, he paid the price. If he succeeded at something, no one could take away the victory as their own. No way he could have that as long as he was around Walt.

The ranch had been Walt's idea, his dream since he

was a young'un. Bart might be mad at him now, but he'd never refuse to help either of his brothers find happiness. He figured he could play along for a few months, let Walt be his bossy self, because he wasn't invested in this project.

Then Walt had gone off and ordered him a catalog bride! The nerve of the man to think he knew what was best for Bart. Just thinking about the position his brother had put him in, and the risk he put Bonnie in, made him angry all over again.

A rabbit darted across his path and Bart shot it easily. It was deader than a door nail, but he was so riled up, he shot it three more times to work out his frustration. It should have made him feel better but it didn't. Picking up the bullet-shredded rabbit only made him feel disappointed in himself. He'd lost control and took it out on this poor creature.

Slowly he headed back to camp, pondering his situation. Something Nate said the night before kept running through his mind but he couldn't quite figure it out. He'd said, "Ain't nobody can make you do nothin' you don't want, deep down."

What was that supposed to mean? Was he suggesting that Bart *wanted* to get married that day? Ridiculous!

Walt had put him in an impossible position. Bonnie was smart enough to come up with a solution that took the pressure off but he honestly wasn't sure what he would have done if she'd expected something more...traditional.

He always liked to think he was a free spirit, a man who could never be tied down, but he wasn't like a lot of drifters he'd met throughout the years. He didn't hustle, cheat or steal. If he couldn't find work and no one invited him to supper, he'd go hungry rather than steal a loaf of bread. Nope, his pa had raised him right, and he never turned his back on his morals, even when he was surrounded by scoundrels.

And that strong sense of right was his downfall. Walt played him like their granddaddy's fiddle and he'd walked headlong into the trap. What else was he supposed to do? Nope, Walt had tricked him into marrying Bonnie, and that was that.

He cleaned and spitted the rabbit in a trice and sat back watching it crisp up. The familiar smell took him back to one of his many adventures, one which involved a scraggly old ship captain with an honest-to-goodness peg leg. Claimed he won it in a card game and that it once belonged to the famous pirate François Leclerc. Bart wasn't buying what the man was trying to sell, but it was a good story so he played along.

Bart caught himself as he was opening his mouth to tell the story to Bonnie so she could write it down. He'd miss telling her stories once he was gone for good. He loved the light in her eye as she scribbled down his tales. Her laugh was light yet hearty, kind of like her bread. That sorta described her, too, now that he thought about it.

Kicking back next to the fire, he watched the stars come out through the thinning leaves. Bonnie was always fascinated with his life outdoors. "What's it like sleeping under the stars," she once asked.

He was taken aback for a minute but then remembered she was a city girl. He did his best to describe the feeling but nothing could compare to doing it. The woman had a way with words, and if she just experienced it, he had no doubt she could do it justice. Maybe he should bring her out here someday...

What?! Where did that idea come from? First of all, this was *his* place. Second of all, she wouldn't be interested in riding all day only to sleep on the hard ground.

Would she?

As he thought on it, he rather suspected she might. She had the brains of a businessman but the heart of an adventurer, and he had to admit that she'd turned things upside down. His finances had never been better accounted for and his cabin was starting to look almost like a home. He didn't even want to think about how he'd already had to loosen his belt two notches from her cooking.

Speaking of food... He pulled the spit from the fire and picked a hunk of meat from the hind leg. Popping it in his mouth, he grimaced. This time he knew. It tasted the same as any other time he'd killed a rabbit on the trail, but it didn't compare to what Bonnie could do with it.

He could almost see her cooking a pot of stew with the critter right there across the fire from him. She'd smile up at him prettily as she dropped a wild onion in the concoction, and the smell would make him think he'd died and gone to heaven.

"Tell me a story, Bart," she would say, and he'd oblige. Maybe he'd add a little color, maybe not, but he'd make sure she ended up laughing. There wasn't a happier sound in the world than Bonnie laughing. Just thinking of it made him smile.

There was no doubt about it, he missed his Bonnie Blue.

-19-

Bonnie laid in bed until light peeked in through the small window in the bedroom. Since Bart wasn't there, she didn't have any reason to get up early. Of course that didn't mean she wasn't awake before dawn.

Since her arrival, she'd grown accustomed to his light snoring in the other room, and now that it was gone, she could barely sleep. Every sound set her on edge, wondering if it was a pack of wild wolves or brazen bandits. At some point during the night, she crept out of her room to grab the shotgun. The sound of an owl hooting sent her scurrying back to her room.

She slept only marginally better with the gun within reach. It still felt strange to be alone in the cabin. She supposed she'd get used to it — she'd have to, because she was certain her brothers-in-law wouldn't want her moving in. They'd send her packing back home to Beckham before they'd allow that.

Lying there in the dark, she wondered where Bart was, and if he was eating enough. He was rail thin when she arrived and her first order of business had been to put some meat on his bones. It was hard to tell under his work clothes but his face appeared fuller since her arrival and this pleased her.

What was she going to make for breakfast? Never in her life had she cooked for just herself. She wasn't sure if she even could. Everything sounded like too much trouble for just her. And the thought of sitting at that tiny table all by herself...

She was going to miss Bart's stories, that much was certain. The notebook she was using to document all his adventures was already half-full. By the time he left the ranch for good, they'd have a bookcase worth.

Her gut twisted up at the thought of the day he would eventually leave so she pushed it away. Fear, she figured. There was no need to be afraid. She'd be just fine on her own. Her parents had always complained about how independent she was, and she would finally be able to put that particular trait to good use.

Lying there in the dim light of the new day, she worked up a plan. She'd have Bart teach her how to shoot all kinds of guns, and she'd practice until she was a sharpshooter. She would take over some of the brothers' chores, such as milking the cows, in exchange for any chores she couldn't do. Maybe she'd set up that sewing business, going to Wiggieville once a week to take orders and deliver finished items.

And she'd learn to cook for one.

Once Libby and Gwen mastered — well, at least had a basic grasp of — cooking, it was time to move on to sewing. Bonnie worried that Gwen would give up after the first time she pricked her finger, but she was pleasantly surprised that her sister seemed fiercely determined to learn the skill. She'd never even had to thread a needle back home.

"I don't know why you made such a fuss, Bonnie," Gwen said proudly holding up her practice swatch. The hem she'd sewn was not only crooked, but the stitches were all different lengths and tension. "Sewing is simple!" Bonnie bit the inside of her cheek to stop herself from laughing.

As usual, Libby concentrated hard on her work, which was much better than Gwen's, but she still ended up dissatisfied. The poor child — woman, Bonnie reminded herself — was always so hard on herself. She hoped Nate wasn't adding to her sister's insecurities. She honestly doubted this was the case, but if he was, she'd have something to say about it, regardless if Libby was his wife.

"Libby, sweetheart, you'll be making the most

beautiful dresses in no time," she soothed, patting Libby's back. Libby smiled up at her uncertainly and went back to her work.

By afternoon, they insisted on putting their new skills to work on curtains for Bonnie's cabin.

"It's just scandalous that anybody could peep into your windows," Gwen exclaimed. Bonnie and Libby exchanged looks and burst out laughing. Gwen frowned at them. "What's so funny?"

Libby was the first to catch her breath. "You? You of all people saying something is scandalous?" That brought on another round of giggles.

Gwen looked perturbed for a moment, then joined them. "How silly!"

The sound of a carriage outside sobered them up quickly. They'd only met a few people in town so far; it seemed unlikely anyone would come calling.

As much as Bonnie wanted to follow Gwen to the door, she and Libby stayed put at the table. It was Gwen's house, after all, and they were guests.

But the moment a woman's voice said, "I'm here to see Walton about our baby," she leapt to her feet. Libby looked confused and slightly terrified.

Gwen handled the situation better than Bonnie would ever have imagined. She told the strange woman, who gave every appearance of being a lady of the night, that she would tell her husband where to find her. After shutting the door on the woman's gawking face, Gwen scurried into her room and stayed there for some time.

Libby moved to follow but Bonnie held her back. "She needs to think right now," she whispered. But she wasn't about to leave her sister alone. So they sat in silence and sewed.

Bonnie's heart broke for Gwen. She was so happy with Walt, and she was trying so hard to be a good wife. Now this. She supposed that was the good thing about not being in love with your spouse — there were no expectations, so there were no disappointments.

Finally, Gwen emerged and announced she would be staying with Bonnie, to which she immediately agreed. It would be nice to have someone in the house with her, though she wasn't happy about the reason.

Bonnie stared at the stove, wondering what to make herself while she waited for Gwen to have it out with Walt. Nothing sounded good. Without someone to cook for, she lost all interest in food. She ended up slathering jam on a stale biscuit and calling it good.

Normally any free time she managed to scrape together during the day was filled with projects, from sewing Gwen's dress to baking to lessons to cleaning. But sitting there waiting for Gwen to arrive, all she could do was stare into the fire. Her eyes drifted over to the pile of wood Bart had left for her and she sighed.

A soft knock pulled her out of her stupor and soon she was comforting and advising Gwen on her marriage. It was exhausting. Besides, what did she know about love and marriage? Both her sisters seemed to think she and Bart were the perfect couple. If they only knew!

It had been years since Bonnie had shared a bed with Gwen, but it comforted them both. Gwen didn't even complain about how small or how hard it was, just crawled in and curled up against her big sister.

Bonnie woke up once in the middle of the night to the sound of Gwen's quiet sobs, but let her be. She was devastated, not only by the prostitute supposedly carrying Walt's child, but that he'd called her by the wrong name. And worst of all, he'd called her Gertie, the name of the woman who spread all the lies about the Blue sisters back in Beckham! Talk about rubbing salt in the wound. She had a mind to give him a tongue-lashing for it.

Poor Gwen! If that's what being in love was all about, Bonnie was glad she wasn't in love.

-20-

Bart didn't want to push Roamer so he decided to break up the trip back to the ranch into two days. He was in no hurry to return because he hoped a little distance would put his current situation into perspective.

Most of the day, Bart walked next to his horse, only riding when Roamer wanted to move a little faster. All that walking gave him a lot of time to think, not to mention sore feet.

He was a drifter, always on the move. That freedom defined him. But something was different inside him. Something had changed and he didn't know what. He was *supposed* to want to get back out on the trail, seeing what he could see, never stopping in the same place twice. So why did he feel so weary at the thought of heading off for good?

He'd done a lot of crazy things in his life, and met some even crazier people. That was part of the allure of being a drifter. But more and more, the craziness wasn't holding his interest. He found it...boring.

Take Winston for example, the drunk he ran into in Wiggieville. That old reprobate had doddled around the west for years, and he had some fantastical stories to tell. But get him talking about anything beyond his mostly made-up adventures, and the man was an embarrassment.

How had Winston turned out so bad? Were the years of never settling in one place to blame, or did he move around because of who he was inside? After their last conversation, Bart had no illusions about the man. He was no good.

Just as were so many others he'd met on the trail. Most of them, really. The 'professional' drifters, anyway. There were a bunch who just played at it for a while before finally settling in one place. All the *real* drifters — which was what Bart had always considered himself — laughed at those fakers, called 'em tenderfoots...or worse.

But the more time he spent with the 'real' drifters, the less he liked them. He'd been raised with a solid sense of right and wrong, but most of the fellas he knew blurred the lines to their liking.

In the beginning, he was blind to it, believing in the fantasy he'd built up around the lifestyle. Then cracks started to form in the façade and he could no longer turn a blind eye to their amoral ways. Now, ten years in, he had no illusions about who his fellow drifters were, which was why he would only ride with others for a short time, never getting involved with their devilry.

Only now, as he walked alongside his faithful companion, did he wonder why he kept going. The traveling was always interesting but also tiresome. He'd met so many wonderful folks, that couldn't be denied, but the one thing that surprised him was that people were the same no matter where he landed. There were good women, bad men and everything in between.

So why did he want to get back out there so badly? Just because he was 'supposed' to? He'd always prided himself on having a mind of his own, never doing what was expected of him. But as he followed the path of his past, he realized that wasn't true.

As the youngest, everyone expected him to be the wild child, so he obliged. The night he left home, he thought everyone would be shocked, but there they were in the barn waiting to say goodbye. Out on the road, people assumed he'd move on sooner or later, and it was usually sooner.

He'd always thought he was searching for something as he drifted around. Was it possible he was running, too? Running from what others wanted him to do or be? And here he was doing it again. Walt wanted him to settle down, but Bart's natural instinct was to run.

Nate's comment kept tickling the back of his brain as he trudged along. *You're a grown man now and ain't nobody can make you do nothin' you don't want, deep down.*

It hit him like a sledgehammer. He stopped cold in his tracks, Roamer halting next to him with a snort. All this time he thought he was being his own man out there on the trail, but he was really just avoiding making any real decisions. He'd let life happen to him, instead of taking the bull by the horns and making his life what he really wanted, deep down.

Nate was right about one thing. He was a grown man. Walt couldn't make him do anything he didn't want to do.

It was time to prove it.

-21-

The prostitute, Lela Mason, returned the next day to apologize to Gwen for lying. When she found herself in desperate straits, she remembered what a good man Walton was, and hoped she could trick him into marrying her.

Then the most amazing thing happened: Gwen, the selfish brat who never cared a whit about others, invited Lela in for tea! Bonnie was floored, and Libby looked downright scandalized.

But after they heard the poor woman's sad tale, they all decided help her. Libby suggested she start a sewing business in Wiggieville, which gave Bonnie pause. That's what she'd been planning for herself, but this woman and her child would need a steady income. Bonnie could just start a different business.

When Libby pointed out there were plenty of single

men looking for a wife, Bonnie had to chime in. "Just make sure you're honest with whomever you choose. I'd hate for a man to marry you only to be upset that you once had a less than desirable lifestyle."

"You girls sure have some interesting ways of avoiding saying I was a whore," Lela said good-naturedly.

Bonnie liked the woman's candid ways. It was refreshing, after a lifetime of watching every word you said. Then Gwen started giggling hysterically.

"I was just thinking about how Mama would react if she knew we'd run away to Texas and were sitting in my new house entertaining a former whore."

Libby gasped at the word, but Bonnie gasped at the idea. "She'd have an apoplectic fit!"

Before parting ways for the night, they vowed to find a situation for Lela in Wiggieville, where no one needed to know about her past.

Naturally, Gwen didn't need to spend the night since she and Walt made up, so Bonnie was once again left facing a cold stove with no motivation to do anything but curl up in bed and sleep.

She felt like she could sleep for days.

A soft knock on her door roused her from drowsing in front of the fireplace. She'd dreamt she was sleeping under a black sky filled with stars, and two warm blankets were wrapped snugly around her, keeping her warm and safe.

She shook the cobwebs from her head, wondering how blankets could keep you safe, but forgot all about it as she went to answer the door. Who could it be? Was it Bart?

Libby stood on the threshold looking worried, as usual. "I need to talk to you before Nate gets home," she said, pushing past Bonnie and perching herself on Bart's crate. Tears spilled down her perfect cheeks.

Good grief, another of her sisters needing emotional support. Why must she always be the rock? Why wasn't anyone ever the rock for her?

"Oh Bonnie, everything's wrong!"

"What do you mean everything? I thought the two of you were..." Her voice caught in her throat when she tried to say 'in love'. Clearing her throat, she tried again, settling for, "I thought you two were fine."

Libby wailed about Nate not loving her but maybe she loved him and how she didn't know how she would live through such a thing. That caught Bonnie's attention. "Live?"

"What I mean is, I don't know how I can live my life married to a man who doesn't love me. It would be easier if I wasn't in love with him, I suppose, but... I think I am. Am I making any sense?"

All the blood in her body rushed to Bonnie's feet, for some reason. Luckily she was standing a step away from her chair and it caught her full weight when her knees buckled. She took a deep cleansing breath and tried to still her shivering frame.

"I'd like to say not any more than usual, but in this case, you make perfect sense."

Libby scooted closer. Bonnie wouldn't meet her gaze or she would see something was wrong. Because something was dreadfully wrong...

"You're in love with Bart," Libby was saying. "What's it like?"

She wasn't in love with Bart! Impossible! If she was, she'd sentenced herself to a fate worse than marrying an old lecher. Because Libby was right; that would be horrible.

Libby was waiting for her answer. A lump formed in her throat and it wouldn't go down. Her heart was beating faster than she could ever remember it beating. What was the question again? Why was Libby tormenting her like this?!

"Like?"

"Yes, what does it feel like? Maybe if I knew the symptoms, I'd be able to tell if I was in love with Nate or not."

Libby went on and on about wooing and falling in love and what that should look like. It took Bonnie a few minutes for her thoughts to clear enough to hear what Libby was saying. She didn't seem to understand what love was about.

"Then what's it about?" she demanded.

Bonnie wasn't sure what to say because she'd never been in love, but the words just started pouring out of her. "Well, it's about doing things for him that you maybe don't want to do, but you're going to do them anyway because you care about him. It's about being alongside him day in and day out, not always because you want to, but because it's the right place to be. It's about taking care of his home and having pride in your work. Part of it's for you, yes, but also for him. It's putting your trust in him, Libby, knowing that he has your best interest in mind and that you can count on..."

A sense of horror washed over her and suddenly she felt faint. All she wanted was for her sister to leave. Through a buzzing in her head, she heard Libby ask if she was all right, but she couldn't answer. All she could do was feel. That needed to stop. Now.

Somehow she muddled through the rest of the conversation but she had no idea what she was saying. The entire time, the same terrible words kept running through her head:

I'm in love with my husband.

Bonnie pressed her back on the door she'd just closed behind Libby. The sound of blood rushing in her ears drowned out the world. She was shaking like a leaf, and when her knees gave out, she slid down the door into a crumpled, heaving pile.

Sobbing on the bare wood, she pressed her hot cheek to its coolness, heedless of splinters. Her breath hitched and shoulders shook as she was overcome with despair. How could she be in love with Bart?! She'd run away from Beckham to avoid a life of misery, only to fall in love with a man who could never love her. It was the worst possible outcome.

Tears flowed freely and pooled under her. She'd never been much of a cryer, but the wall she'd spent her whole life building was crumbling around her, leaving her vulnerable. She hated it.

All those times she'd had crushes on boys who didn't know she even existed were nothing compared to her feelings for Bart. How could she make such a mistake as to let her defenses down with him? How had she not seen that she was falling for him? After her talk with Libby, there wasn't a shred of doubt in her mind that she was in love. Madly, deeply, head-over-heels in love.

Looking back, she recognized the signs. She woke up early every morning, more chipper and eager to please him than the day before. Without even knowing it, she tried to top herself with every meal she fed him, hoping to impress him. Whenever he told a funny story or a joke, she giggled like a schoolgirl. And when he touched her...oh, how she longed for those moments.

From the moment she met him, she knew Bart was a good man, even if he was a drifter and habitually tardy. He'd taken great pains to make sure she knew who and what he was because he didn't want her getting any funny ideas about a future together. He was quite clear that was never going to happen, and she admired him for his honesty. Many men might have been tempted to take advantage of the situation, leaving her high and dry later. Not Bart. He was a man of integrity.

She couldn't pretend to understand his desire to never settle down, but she respected it. His stories of the adventures he'd had were thrilling, and the idea of spending the night under a great black sky sounded quite romantic. Of course, if it were her, she'd want someplace to call home, too.

But it wasn't her, and he wasn't asking her to join him. He was his own man and he moved around for his own reasons. Reasons she would never fully comprehend.

Her tears finally ran out, leaving Bonnie exhausted on the floor. She imagined the broken wall of bricks guarding her heart and picked up a trowel. If she was going to live the rest of her life in love with a man who didn't love her — and who would most likely be gone within months — she'd better start patching that wall back up.

Slowly, she pulled herself together and stood.

Swaying in the middle of the nearly empty cabin, she took a deep breath and let the chill of her reality fill her down to her toes.

The last thing Bonnie Blue would ever do was give up, so she would just have to adapt. And to adapt she had to live. And to live she had to eat. Yes, the first thing she needed to do was finally make herself a meal.

A meal for one.

-21-

Light was just starting to brighten the night sky by the time Bonnie fell asleep. She couldn't rightly call it sleep, more like an exhausted stupor. She woke hours later, barely refreshed at all. A glance out the bedroom window revealed gray skies that reflected her mood.

She had no idea what time it was but it had to be mid-morning by now. If she was going to get back into a routine — one that didn't include Bart — she was going to have to start by waking at a more reasonable hour.

Today she would bake for herself, and talk to Walt and Nate about trading household chores. If she kept teaching their wives how to become better cooks, there was no doubt they would agree to whatever she wanted.

This was cold comfort because she could never have what she really wanted. He was out on the prairie somewhere, probably not even thinking twice about her.

Another brick was set in place.

Moving into the kitchen, she stoked the fire in the stove. She lit it the night before and was determined to keep it hot. The way she lost her appetite after Bart left frightened her a little, and she didn't want to let it happen again.

She'd tried to cook a small meal, just for herself, but naturally she overdid it. Venison stew would be on the menu for days, but that didn't bother her much. She would get the hang of it eventually, and maybe on the odd days she made extra, she could invite the others over.

Speaking of, she was rather surprised one or the other of her sisters hadn't demanded her attention and time this morning. If she wasn't at one of their homes early, they were hustling over to fetch her to fix some disaster or teach them how to sweep the floor. Nate and Walt were almost certainly out working, so maybe they were finally doing things on their own.

Suddenly she missed their company. All her life, she'd been surrounded by family, rarely getting any time to herself. Naturally she cherished those quiet moments, and she would often take long walks alone. But standing there in the tiny cabin, she'd never felt more lonely in her life.

Telltale pinpricks behind her eyes warned of tears. Shaking her head, she poured herself a cup of coffee and sat in the cabin's sole chair. She'd meant to meet with Mr. Standish, the furniture maker, when they'd gone to town, but in all the hustle and bustle, she completely forgot. Maybe she didn't need anything more than this, since it would soon be just her in the place.

Tears threatened again but she sniffed them away. This was what she'd always wanted! A life of an independent woman. Maybe she'd write a book about her own life one day! A sigh of defeat escaped her lips. She wasn't really believing it yet, but maybe one day she would.

The sound of a wagon brought her to her feet. Bart? No, it couldn't be. He only took Roamer when he left. This was someone else.

Before the horses came to a stop outside her door, she was setting the shotgun just inside it. She didn't want to be inhospitable, but she was a lone woman out on the prairie with no men around. If anything bad was going to happen, she wanted to be prepared.

Swinging the door wide, Bonnie could only gape at what she saw. Mr. Standish and another man were perched on the seat of his wagon, smiling at her. The back was packed with a variety of furniture pieces, each more beautiful than the next. Hopping down, he tipped his hat at her.

"Howdy, ma'am. Reckon you've been chomping at the bit to get this order. I wish I coulda got 'em to ya sooner, but I only had so much already made."

"I...what is all this?" she asked.

Mr. Standish looked amused. "Bart didn't tell ya? Guess he wanted to surprise his new bride. Ain't that sweet, Mitch?"

Mitch, a big man with a quiet nature, nodded and began unloading the wagon. There was a full-sized table and set of six chairs, a beautiful kitchen sideboard, a rocking chair and...was that a bed?

"Mr. Standish, I don't understand," she said, following as the men lugged the table inside.

"Where do you want it, Mrs. Dalton?" he asked, panting with exertion. It was a big table. Not knowing what else to do, she pointed where Bart's homemade table sat.

"Thought Bart woulda told ya. He ordered up this lot here just before church started. I already had all of it 'cept the chairs. He insisted on six chairs instead of just four. Told him it'd take a week. Hope you don't mind."

"Bart did this?" She could barely hear her own voice.

"Sure did," he said, walking back out for another load.

The men hustled in and out, moving the load into the cabin, leaving Bonnie to stand in awe as her little shack turned into a home almost instantly. She couldn't have been more pleased with the furniture and her heart swelled that Bart had been so thoughtful to place the order.

Try as she might, she couldn't stop a few tears from spilling, so she hurried into the kitchen to make some coffee for Mr. Standish and his man Mitch. She didn't want them to see her crying so she kept her back turned when one of them came tromping back into the house.

"I hope you'll stay for a cup of coffee before you go," she called out.

"I just get home and you're already kicking me out?"

Bonnie almost dropped the pot at the sound of Bart's amused tone. Whipping around, she lost the ability to think when she saw him leaning his back against the door jamb, one boot kicked up behind him, and a broad smile on his handsome, scruffy face. That darn wall was shaking like it was in an earthquake, and so was she.

Turing back to the stove, she busied herself, not daring to look at him. What was her life going to be like if he had this effect on her every time he walked in the room? Maybe she'd be better off running back home, getting an annulment and marrying that old geezer. The thought churned her stomach.

"Welcome back," she said more stonily than she intended. She had to shore up her failing wall.

"It's good to see ya, Bonnie Blue," he said, pushing away from the door and moving toward her, his boots clumping on the floor.

She didn't know what to say. Of course it was good to see him, too, but she didn't dare say such a thing. But she had to say something...anything.

"You forgot to take off your boots," she finally whispered.

He paused for a moment, then chuckled. "What do ya know." He resumed his slow walk toward the kitchen.

All the while, Bonnie kept her head down, focusing on the brewing coffee. This was torment! She wanted nothing more than to fly into his arms, to tell him how she felt, but she wouldn't be able to survive the rejection that was sure to come.

"You're back early," she finally squeaked out. "I wasn't expecting you for a week."

"Yeah?"

She jumped at how close his voice was behind her. Slowly she turned to face him. She didn't want to but it seemed she was powerless to resist. Looking up into his deep brown eyes sent shivers throughout her body. Blinking madly, she nodded. "Uh huh..." she sighed.

He stepped closer to her, never moving his gaze from hers. They were inches apart and her insides felt like the raging rapids of a river. What was he doing?

"Did you miss me?" he murmured, one hand

reaching up to stroke a stray hair from her forehead. His finger traced a slow line down her cheek to her neck. She couldn't stop the shudder that wracked her small frame.

She also couldn't stop from nodding slightly. "Uh huh..." she sighed again.

A sweet smile touched his lips ever so slightly. "That's good to hear. Cuz I missed you somethin' awful, Bonnie Blue."

His gaze dropped to her lips and hers did the same as he lowered his head toward hers. Was this really happening? Was he really going to kiss her?

"That's the last of it, Mrs. Dalt—" Mr. Standish stopped at the threshold. Bonnie gasped and pulled away from Bart, spinning back around to the stove. Bart sighed behind her.

"Oh, sorry for interrupting! Bart, good to see ya. I left the bill on the table. Bye now!" He ran out of the cabin and rode his team away.

The tension in the kitchen was thicker than butter on Christmas Day. Bonnie fiddled around with the coffee, hoping Bart would go sit at their new table but he just leaned against the kitchen entryway, watching her.

"Coffee?" she asked. It seemed she could only find one word at a time.

"I'd rather have something sweeter," he said, his tone teasing. She blushed furiously at his overt flirting. He'd never done that before. If she was going to survive his coming and going, she'd have to put a stop to that.

Clenching her jaw, she turned to stare him down. "Bart, you listen here—"

He thrust a box at her. It was flat and made of some kind of beautiful exotic wood, expertly varnished. She blinked in confusion. "What's this?"

One side of his mouth tilted up in a smirk. "Consider it a wedding present."

She frowned at that. It wasn't seemly to make light of marriage, but she couldn't totally blame him. This sham had been her idea, after all. As much as she thought a wedding present was inappropriate under the circumstances, she was curious to find out what was inside the exquisite case.

Unfastening the shiny brass catch, she thumbed it open and gasped. Lying in individual indentations in a bed of dark red velvet was the tortoise-shell hair set she'd fallen in love with at the mercantile. Bonnie was speechless, her gaze flicking between him and the hair set. How did he know?

Stepping forward again, Bart grabbed her shoulders, desperation twisting his handsome features. "Bonnie, I've spent my whole life wandering around looking for something. I never knew what it was till I met you. The first time I laid eyes on you, I was smitten, only I didn't know it. I thought I knew what I wanted," he said, shaking his head in disgust. "I was a bigger hard-headed fool than Walt!"

"I don't understand." She truly didn't.

He took the case and set it on the new sideboard, taking her limp hands in his. It seemed impossible that her heart could beat any faster than it was, but when he crouched down on one knee and looked up at her, his face open and loving, she thought it might pound right out of her chest.

"Bonnie Blue, I love you with all my heart. When you came to live here, you turned an empty ol' shack into a home full of love and laughter. And you turned this empty ol' drifter into a man. I'm nothin' without you, Bonnie. I know this was supposed to be a business arrangement and all that, but..."

He paused and took a deep breath. "Will you do me the honor of being my wife...for real?"

Tears spilled freely down her face but she paid them no mind. The man of her dreams, the love of her life was offering her the world. Why was she hesitating? She finally found the words.

"What about your travels? Your adventures? Bart, you have no idea how much I want to accept what you're offering but...if you left, it would break me."

Bart leapt to his feet and gathered her in his arms. They were as warm and comforting as the finest wool blankets. She pressed her face to his chest and breathed him in.

"Bonnie Blue, you got cotton in your ears, girl? I'm half a man without you. I don't want to step foot off this ranch unless you're by my side. Just imagine all the adventures we could have together!"

Bonnie pulled back. "Together? You want me to go with you on your safaris?"

Cupping her face in his hands, he said, "You're my wife. I want you with me always. Whaddya say?"

He searched her face as he waited for her answer. But there was only one answer. Nodding and blinking away her tears, she nearly shouted, "Yes!"

He grinned and hugged her tight, twirling her in a circle. Setting her back on her feet, he cupped her face again, lowering his until his lips were just an inch from hers. His hot breath made her dizzy and she couldn't wait for their first true kiss.

"Hoo boy, this has been a long time coming," he whispered.

Tears brightened her eyes as she smiled at him. "Better late than never."

-Epilogue-

The Dalton Ranch, Christmas Day, 1888

Bart had never been happier. All those years, he'd laughed at the drifters who settled in one place, but now he was proud to join their ranks. He had the smartest, most beautiful wife in the world, and the Dalton Empire, as Walt liked to call it, was thriving. It wasn't big yet, but it was growing by leaps and bounds every day.

So was his sister-in-law Gwen's belly. She and Walt were over the moon with joy that Gwen was expecting, and Bart suspected that some of their pride involved being the first Daltons to have a baby. Walt always liked to be the best at everything.

And for the first time in his life, Bart was completely fine with it.

"That was a fine meal Libby, Gwen," Nate mumbled through a mouthful of food, patting his stomach. "I don't know when I've eaten as much."

"And to think we had no help from Bonnie!" Gwen said proudly.

Bart smiled noncommittally because, as delicious as the meal was, it couldn't compare to anything Bonnie had ever made him. But he had to admit that her sisters had taken her lessons to heart, and they were very good students.

"You're a wonderful cook," Walt was saying to Gwen. "I can't wait for you to teach our...well, whatever it is we're having."

"Even if it's a boy?" asked Bart, trying to needle his older brother a little.

"Even if it's a boy," Walt said with a smile.

Out of the corner of his eye, he saw Libby fidgeting in her chair. Before he could think twice about it, Bonnie spoke up.

"Who's ready for dessert?"

Dessert?! Bonnie made the best pies on earth. It was all she could do to keep him out of them as they cooled on the sideboard earlier in the day. But she was a smart woman and distracted him in other, much more pleasing ways.

"You know I am!" he and Walt in unison. There was a moment's pause, then everyone burst out laughing. In fact, they were laughing so loud, no one even noticed when the door was thrown open.

Walt spotted the intruders first. He came halfway out of his chair and barely had time to say "What the..." before the very distinct sounds of shotguns being cocked stopped him.

Three very angry-looking men stood in the doorway. Bart didn't take his eyes off them, even when Gwen leapt to her feet and screeched at them.

"Benedict! What are you doing here?!"

But when Bonnie gasped and said, "Hank?" Bart had no choice but to gawk at his wife. "Who the hel—"

He was interrupted by Libby squeaking out the third man's name. "Percy?"

The Dalton brothers were caught off guard. They had no guns at the ready, no weapons...and the fact that their wives knew these men, was the most disarming of all!

"Get em up," demanded the first one, Benedict. "Now!"

Bart exchanged glances with his brothers but they were at a distinct disadvantage, so raised their hands in the air.

"Gwen, Libby, Bonnie," said the one in the middle. Hank, was it? "Get over here. We're...taking you home."

Bonnie stood beside him. What was she doing? Was she really going with these villains?

"Hank? What in heaven's name are you doing

here?"

How did she know this man? His head felt like it would explode with all the unanswered questions swimming around in it.

"We might ask you the same question!" snapped the third man, Percy.

"If you must know," Gwen said, "we live here!"

"Yes, we can see that," Benedict said, taking a threatening step forward. "And it looks mighty cozy."

If he wasn't so angry and afraid at the same time, Bart would have felt sympathy for poor little Libby. She looked terrified.

"You can't take us back!" she screamed. "You just can't!"

It was Nate's turn to get angry. "Take you back? What are you talking about? Who are these men?"

"We'd like to know the same about you!" Percy spit out as he raised his shotgun a little higher. Bart watched his every movement and could see he wasn't comfortable with a gun. That was good.

"I don't care who you are!" barked Walt. "You're trespassing, get off our land!"

"You're hardly in a position to demand anything," Hank pointed out. "All we want are these women."

All they wanted were their wives? Were these men insane or just stupid?

"Yeah, they've caused us a lot of trouble the last few months!" added Benedict.

"How could we?" asked Gwen. "We've been here the whole time!"

"Precisely," agreed Percy, leveling his gun unsteadily at Nate's chest. "Which is why we've come to fetch you and take you back to where and whom you belong,"

"Percy! Don't!" Libby cried.

"Don't what? Shoot this scum for running off with ya? Or was it the other way around?"

Libby threw herself in front of Nate, who shoved her behind him. Good man, thought Bart. He was about to do the same with Bonnie, when she shouted.

"Enough!"

Silence descended on the scene for a moment. Hank stepped forward slightly, a contrite look on his face. "Bonnie, please. We have to do this."

Bart didn't care who these men were any more. No one was taking his wife. He's spent too long searching for her and he'd kill anyone who came between them.

"Shut up, all of you!" Bart shouted.

"I say we hang these scum," hissed Percy.

All three sisters were now on their feet. "No!"

And then, all hell broke loose...

Bonnie stood stock still as Nate and Libby's cabin turned into a brawl rivaled only by the seediest of western saloons. Walt pushed Gwen behind him, no doubt in an effort to protect her but it only sent her sprawling into a corner. Libby disappeared beneath the table, frightened as a kitten, while all three Dalton brothers lunged for her brothers.

Thankfully, the Dalton brothers quickly evened the odds. Bart wrested Benedict's gun from his hands while Walt went for Hank. Percy had never taken to using a gun, though he talked a big game, so it only took one glancing blow from Nate for him to drop it.

Terrified that one of them — a Blue or a Dalton — might shoot one of the others, she ran between men to scoop up the shotguns. Someone's elbow connected with the side of her head and nearly knocked her down.

There was movement everywhere. Fists flew and clothing tore. She'd never heard such cursing before! What were all these foolish boys thinking?

The bigger question was, how had they tracked them down? She was half in shock at their arrival and half in shock at the scene of chaos before her. Had Hank blabbed, as she'd feared he would? He'd seemed so sincere in wanting to help them escape their fate, but now he was here, trying to take them back. It didn't make sense.

Nate screamed in pain and Bonnie saw a small, pale hand yank a knife out of his boot. Libby was trying to stop this melee, poor thing. Poor, brave girl. Bonnie's blood started to boil at what these ridiculous men were doing to her sister's home.

Walt and Hank were pounding on each other, Percy almost got the better of Nate when Libby accidentally stabbed him in the foot, and then Benedict landed a solid blow that sent Bart sprawling to the floor. She heard him ask Libby if she was okay, and then Ben was yanking him back to his feet, his fist cocked to smash him in the face.

Bonnie had seen enough. Grabbing one of the shotguns, she aimed it toward the roof and fired.

BLAM!

Every man in the room froze. They all slowly turned to find the source of the gunshot and gaped when they saw her holding the smoking shotgun. Except Bart. He grinned.

"Sit down, all of you!" Her tone was not one to be argued with but Bossy Ben just had to try.

"Put that gun away before you shoot somebody," he barked.

She'd had enough of his lip for a lifetime. "That's a good idea, maybe I ought to," she said, dropping the barrel in his direction. She took great satisfaction at the look of shock on his face.

Benedict's hands shot up, as did Walt's. Bonnie loved both of them, she really did, but she'd be darned if she'd let these men — no, boys — ruin her first Christmas with Bart.

"Walt! She's not going to shoot you!" Gwen

screeched, running to him..

Walt pulled Gwen into his arms and turned toward her brothers. "Who are you?

"We're the Blue brothers," said Hank. "And we've come to take our sisters home."

"Brothers?" Nate pulled Libby to him. "You never said you had brothers."

"And our sisters never said they were leaving," added Percy in his usual snide tone.

Bart's head bobbed between them. "Leaving? What do ya mean, leaving?"

"He means our sisters ran out on a scandal caused by Gwen," Ben huffed. "To alleviate any further damage to the family name, our father painstakingly chose a husband for each of them."

"Yeah, and how do they show their appreciation?" sneered Percy. "By running away. Pa sent us here to bring you back. Deacons Smith, Bellafonte and Jackson paid a tidy sum for us to do it, too."

"But you can't take us back," Gwen cried.

"And why not?" Benedict pretended he was focusing on Gwen, but Bonnie could see he was inching closer to her. Did he really think he'd get the gun from her. Silly boy.

"Because we're all married, that's why." Bonnie said, raising the gun higher.

He glared at her but at least he stopped moving. "We figured that might happen, but the deacons don't care. They want you three like fleas want a dog."

Libby and Gwen gasped. Bonnie thought she might be sick. How could their brothers think they'd leave their husbands?

"If you're thinking that we're getting annulments, you're sadly mistaken," said Gwen, as if reading Bonnie's mind.

Percy shrugged. "It's been done before. I just hope these scum haven't dishonored you beyond repair."

Bonnie almost shot him right there for saying such things. Gwen just rolled her eyes at him. "They've done nothing of the sort. In fact, I'm not only married, I'm expecting!"

All the Blue boys shifted their gazes to her belly. "You're lying," said Ben, his tone not at all confident.

"No, I'm not."

Percy leaned over toward Ben. "So what if we only bring back two. Two out of three ain't bad."

"Oh, no you won't," Libby cried.

This time Hank chimed in. "And why not?" Bonnie leveled her angriest glare on him and he shuffled his feet like a little boy caught being naughty.

"Because I'm going to have a baby, too."

Libby was pregnant, too? Bonnie wanted to cry with joy. Nate, too, from the sound of his voice.

"What? You are? Good God, Libby, are ya sure?"

"Yeah, are ya sure?" Ben asked, looking as pale as Nate.

"I'm sure."

"Libby, my little Libby..."

Even with everything going on, Libby looked euphoric. So did Nate, and who could blame them. It would have been a touching scene if Percy hadn't chosen that moment to pipe up.

"Looks like it's just you, Bonnie."

"I don't know what those deacons paid you to bring us back, but I'm not going."

"Put the gun down, Bonnie," Hank said, his voice low. "Let's talk about this. We...we can't go back empty handed."

"Why not?" He paused so she shifted the barrel his direction to jog his memory.

"Because..."

"Quiet!" snapped Percy. "Let's just take her and go."

"You're not taking my wife anywhere," growled Bart. "Bonnie, give me that gun."

"No."

Just who did he think he was talking to? And why was everyone staring at her?

"What?"

"I said no. These are our brothers, Bart, and they wouldn't be acting so desperate without a good reason."

"I'll not let them take you..."

"You don't have to. I can't go either."

He blanched at her words, unsure of her meaning but clearly hoping. He took a step toward her. "Bonnie…"

"I'm expecting, too."

"What?" Gwen and Libby squealed loud enough to make her ears bleed. "Bonnie!"

"Bonnie?" Bart whispered. She smiled at him sweetly, wishing fervently that she could run into his arms and celebrate the happy news. But she had other fish to fry at the moment.

"So you see, my dear brothers, you've failed as far as taking us back. Now the only question I have for you, is, what are you really doing here?"

~ THE END ~

The Drifter's Mail-Order Bride is part of *The Dalton Brides* series. Read on for excerpts from two other books in the series:

The Rancher's Mail-Order Bride
by Kirsten Osbourne

&

The Cowboy's Mail-Order Bride
by Kit Morgan

THE RANCHER'S MAIL ORDER BRIDE
by
Kirsten Osbourne

Through no fault of her own, Gwen Blue found herself embroiled in a scandal that would set Beckham, Massachusetts on its ear, and get her locked in her room for two months. When she found herself betrothed to a man she found loathsome, she wanted nothing more than to disappear. When her sisters liberated her from her room and proposed a journey to Texas to visit an old school friend, she didn't have to be asked twice.

Walton Dalton always had a plan for his life. He'd spent years learning everything he needed to know about ranching, and he had a large parcel of land adjacent to his two brothers' land. Between the three of them, they were going to build a Texas ranching empire. For his empire, he needed a bride.

Without his brothers' knowledge, Walt sends off for three mail order brides from a matchmaker in Beckham. He knows from the moment he sees

'Gorgeous Gwen' that she's meant to be his. Will she agree to the marriage? If she does, will she be able to get over her self-centered attitude and be a good wife?

EXCERPT

Gwen rushed off the train and immediately started looking around for the stagecoach. Bonnie caught up to her, putting her hand on her sister's shoulder. "Don't run off now!"

"I'm looking for the stagecoach. It's only another three hours, and we'll be there. I can't wait to see Anna." Really, it wasn't so much seeing Anna that she cared about. She needed to be in one place for a while. The journey had been much too long for her.

"You didn't even like Anna," Bonnie argued.

"Well, I love her today, because she's going to let me sleep in a bed that doesn't move!" Gwen looked at Bonnie. "The bed won't move will it? She doesn't live on a boat or something silly like that?"

Bonnie laughed. "No, I don't think the bed will move." She led the way to the platform. "We need to wait for our trunk to be unloaded."

Gwen laughed. "I was so excited to be on the stagecoach, I forgot all about my trunk. That was silly of me, wasn't it?"

Libby and Bonnie exchanged looks. "Our trunk, Gwenny. We could only pack one trunk for the three of us or Mama and Papa would have gotten suspicious."

"Are you serious? You'd better have packed my cornflower blue dress. It's my favorite." Gwen looked between her sisters.

Bonnie sighed. "We couldn't. We didn't have access to your clothes at all, because you were locked in your room, remember? We brought some of Libby's dresses for you."

Gwen made a face. "Libby's dresses? But Libby and I don't look good in the same colors. I'm blond, and Libby's a brunette." Besides, she wanted her own clothes. Clothes that had been made just for her.

"I'll make you a new cornflower blue dress, Gwen. I promise. Just...don't make a fuss."

Gwen looked at her sister, surprised by her words. "A fuss? Why would I make a fuss?" She could see by Bonnie's face something was still wrong. "What were you going to tell me?"

Bonnie sighed. "Well, we're not exactly here to see Anna."

Gwen raised an eyebrow, more than a little annoyed her sisters had lied to her. "Why are we here then?"

"I..." Bonnie avoided Gwen's gaze, something she'd never done.

It must be bad, Gwen thought. If Bonnie can't tell me what's going on, she's done something terrible.

At that moment two men, who were obviously twin brothers, stepped between them. "Are you ladies the Blue sisters?" one of them asked. He had brown eyes and black hair. His shoulders were the broadest she'd ever seen. She wouldn't mind stepping out with him at all.

Gwen nodded slowly. "Who are you?" She'd never seen these men in her life. Why were they looking for them? Were they there to drive them to their new home, wherever it may be? She still didn't know why they were in Texas.

The man who'd asked the question grinned. "I'm Walton Dalton, and I pick you." He grabbed her hand and pulled her into his arms before she had a chance to reply. His mouth covered hers and he kissed her, right there in the middle of the train station.

Gwen stomped on his foot, enjoying the kiss, but she knew it wasn't proper to kiss a man she'd just met. "Unhand me!" She wiped her hand across her mouth, trying to stop the tingling that had started as soon as his lips had met hers.

Walt smiled down at Gwen. "I'll unhand you for now. Preacher's standing by." He kept his arm firmly around his little fiancé's shoulders. "Which sister are you?"

"I'm Gwendolyn. Why do you persist in touching me? I don't know you!" She struggled against him, but realized it was futile. He was much stronger than she would ever be.

Bonnie smiled at Walt. "I'm Bonnie. I'm the oldest sister. I believe I'm the one you're supposed to marry."

Walt looked back and forth between the sisters. "I don't care who's oldest. I'm marrying this one." He nodded at Nate. "That's my brother Nate. Bart should be here by now, but I'm sure he'll be along." He'd better be along. He'd promised Walt he'd be there by three. It was quarter after.

Bonnie glared at Walt and turned to Nate, who was openly staring at Libby. "Libby's the youngest," she announced, seeming to think that would matter to the brothers.

Nate looked back and forth between Walt and Bonnie. "I thought we were here to see a man about some cattle."

Walt grinned at his brother. "Surprise! Since Bart isn't here, you get next pick. Which one do you want for your bride?" He didn't expect a lot of problems from Nate. Bart was the one who would protest the loudest.

Nate blinked. "You sent off for brides for us? The cattle salesman was a lie?"

Walt shrugged. "I didn't think you'd come if I told you why we were really here." He kissed the top of Gwen's head as if they'd been in love for years. "Pick one." He wasn't letting this little beauty go. He'd expected all three sisters to be homely. Gwen had been a fabulous surprise.

Nate pointed at Libby. "I guess I'll take the youngest." He leaned close to Walt and whispered,

"I'll take care of you later."

Gwen gasped in shock. "You can't just pick me and say you'll marry me. No! What on earth is happening here. Bonnie? What have you done?" As grateful as Gwen was to her sister for rescuing her, she was furious about this arrangement. She had no desire to marry a stranger or anyone else for that matter.

Bonnie blinked as if fighting tears. "Libby knew why we were here. We just didn't want you to be stubborn. We rescued you after all."

THE COWBOY'S MAIL ORDER BRIDE
by
Kit Morgan

Libby Blue lived in the shadow of her sister's accomplishments. Bonnie, the oldest, excelled at all things domestic and was the smartest of the three. Gwen, the middle sister, excelled at ... well, Gwen was beautiful, so she didn't have to excel at much else to get what she wanted. Libby tried as hard as she could to live up to both, but always seemed to fall short. But when Gwen is caught up in a major scandal, their father decides to marry Libby and her sisters off to the most un-eligible bachelors in Beckham to save the family's reputation. Bonnie quickly devises a plan to escape their father's wrath and sets it in motion. Libby might yet have a chance to prove herself! As a Mail-Order Bride!

Walton Dalton had a dream to build an empire. Or in this case, a ranch where he and his two brothers could work hard and love hard. Determined to see his dream come true, he sends for his brothers and they soon join him in Texas to claim the land and begin building. That took care of the 'work' part. But Walton fails to tell his brothers that he already sent for mail-order brides in order to take care of the 'loving' part. Will Nate Dalton become Libby's road to happiness? Or a slow path to misery because she still can't measure up?

EXCERPT

Nate took care of the horses, fed the chickens, and was heading back to the house when he stopped dead in his tracks. What would happen now? She couldn't cook, was frightened, and, as far as he knew, didn't like this whole arrangement. He stood, fists on hips and stared at the soft lantern light coming from the windows. Maybe she was upset because she was so ill-prepared to be a wife. How would he feel if he was in her shoes? But then, what woman becomes a wife and doesn't learn how to cook? What else would she be inept at? What if she couldn't so much as mend a shirt, or wash it for that matter? He couldn't exactly send her back. But then, what if that's exactly what she wanted him to do?

Nate rubbed his chin with his hand. How to handle her... that was the question. Should he be patient, or tell her to get with it? Maybe a little of both? Yet, what right did he have to be so hard on her their first day as husband and wife? She did just travel over a thousand miles to get there and must be plumb tuckered out. If he was any kind of a gentleman, he'd get a tub ready for her, let her have her privacy, then after she felt better, he could see where she really stood. Yes, that's what he'd do. He wouldn't be surprised if he found her passed out from exhaustion.

Sure enough, when he entered the house, she was curled up at one end of the settee, eyes closed, breathing steady and even. He studied her in the lantern light. How was he going to turn this delicate flower into someone capable of defending herself and their land if need be? This was still rough country, and he and his brothers could be gone long hours during the day. She'd be alone all that time, as would her sisters. They might have to do whatever was necessary to defend themselves. Could she shoot a gun? Could she, would she, shoot a man if she had to? He crossed to the stove and pushed the thought aside. He'd worry about teaching her how to shoot later. Right now he figured he'd help make things more comfortable for her. Tomorrow was going to be a long day.

He got a fire in the cook stove going, fetched the tub he used for bathing and set it up in the bedroom. He then went out to the pump, got a couple buckets of water, and poured them into the tub. He then filled the buckets again, and put them on the stove to heat.

While he waited he sat at the kitchen table and stared at the back of the settee. He tried to imagine the two of them sitting there in the evenings after supper in front of the fire. He'd read a book, she'd knit or something. After awhile, they'd maybe get sleepy, then again, maybe not. Nate swallowed hard and stood. He took a few steps in her direction, and gazed at the back of her head resting on the one pillow he had for the living area. Her dark hair was coming loose from its pins, and a long tendril escaped, spilling over the arm of the settee. He went to her, reached down, and touched the silken lock. His body reacted, and he let go, sucking in a breath as he did. Libby didn't stir, and he sighed in relief.

Once again, he had to concede to her beauty. But how was she going to survive while he was gone all day? He didn't talk much during the ride home, but he listened. Her sister Bonnie asked him if the land around Bart's home would support a vegetable garden come spring. He told her yes, and knew she wanted to have one so there'd be enough food to get them through next winter. She knew how to cook and preserve food, a good thing in these parts. Bart was one lucky son of a ...

Libby moaned in her sleep. Nate froze. He sucked in another breath, and slowly backed away. He should wake her now, get her something to eat, then leave her to bathe.

He went back to the kitchen. He had some cold bacon from his breakfast left, and a few biscuits. They would have to do for supper. He cut a biscuit in half, slapped a couple pieces of bacon on it, then went to wake his sleeping wife.

He gave her shoulder a shake, and almost jumped when she popped up with a yelp. "Whoa, there," he said in a soft voice. "I didn't mean to scare ya."

She stared at him, her mouth half-open. "Wha... what?" She glanced around the cabin. "What happened?"

"You dozed off. Here, I rustled us up something to eat," he said and handed her the biscuit. She looked at it, then at him. "What is it?"

"Just eat, you'll need something in your belly or you'll be worthless in the morning."

"Worthless?" she whispered. "I see." She took the biscuit from him, studied it, and took a small bite.

"I done fixed you a bath. You can get cleaned up before you turn in. I don't imagine you'd want to sleep in a clean bed unless you're the same."

She raised her eyes to his. "Understood," she said through gritted teeth.

Good grief! What was ailing her now? "I'll be out in the barn." He went to the stove, checked the water, then using a couple of dishrags, plucked the buckets off and added them to the tub in the bedroom. Maybe after she got cleaned up she wouldn't be so... well, whatever it was she was being! All he knew was he didn't care for it. If she was going to be the kind of woman that was hard to please, then this arrangement wasn't going to be to his liking. At least not until she learned what was what.

"I'm going to the barn. I'll be back in an hour." He didn't mean to slam the door on his way out, but he did. Some wedding night this was turning out to be.

CASSIE HAYES

ABOUT THE AUTHOR

Cassie Hayes grew up pretending she was Laura Ingalls (before that pesky Almonzo arrived on the scene) in the middle of Oregon farm country. She lives with her husband and cat on the Pacific Ocean and loves to hear from her readers.

Connect with her at www.CassieHayes.com, Facebook (fb.me/authorcassiehayes) and Goodreads, or by email at authorcassiehayes@gmail.com.

If you enjoy historical western romances, join the Pioneer Hearts group on Facebook at www.facebook. com/groups/pioneerhearts.

Made in the USA
Columbia, SC
01 September 2022

66507395R00138